# STUMBL

Her hand smoothed my trouser leg. I felt in imminent danger of a seizure.

But Mrs Murphy, Maeve, moved not an inch from me on the couch. Her hand still on my leg, her eyes round and rapturously fixed on mine, she sighed rather than spoke.

'Now Father, I know how hard it is for you young priests. You've no one to talk to, no one to share your problems with. So any time you're lonely, any time you want a bit of comfort, you just come on up here. Tom's out most of the day on his doctoring, so I'm nearly always here on my own. Won't that be nice?'

I sat transfixed, my mouth opening and closing like a landed fish.

'Hargh,' I gurgled . . .

# STUMBLING IN THE AISLES

Dermot Kennedy

A STAR BOOK

*published by*
the Paperback Division of
W. H. ALLEN & Co. Ltd

A Star Book
Published in 1979
by the Paperback Division of
W. H. Allen & Co. Ltd
A Howard and Wyndham Company
44 Hill Street, London W1X 8LB



Printed in Great Britain by
C. Nicholls & Company Ltd, The Philips Park Press, Manchester

ISBN 0 352 30343 3

THIS BOOK IS FOR TIM

# CHAPTER ONE

I FELL into Brimley. As the train pulled into the dingy, darkening station, the door I was holding swung open and deposited both me and my suitcase on the platform. My glasses fell from my nose, my new homburg hat skidded and rolled and dropped on to the parallel railway line. Tears, partly of embarrassment, partly of pain came to my eyes as my chin made firm and noisy contact with the flat paving stones.

'Something should be done about those doors. A positive danger.' The strident voice proceeded from a large amorphous matron who was stepping daintily over my prostrate body. 'What's the Church going to do about that?' she bellowed triumphantly as she sailed on down the platform.

I scurried to my feet, whimpering gently. My glasses, though rimless, were unbroken. A couple of ungainly lopes, a leap, and I was down on the other track collecting my muddied homburg. Another roar greeted me as I popped up from the track like a jack-in-the-box. The guard moving down the platform had sprawled full length as he tripped over my suitcase, which was still lying where I had left it.

'Who the bloody hell . . . ?' he began with an air of outrage which promised even more choice language.

'I'm very sorry,' I babbled, only the upper quarter of me visible above the platform. 'I had to get my hat. Sorry about the case. Anything I can do?'

The guard slowly pressed himself upwards. With great care he brushed down his dirtied uniform, looked painfully at his hands and then walked across with great deliberation to where I stood, still on the track. He looked so angry that I thought he might kick me in the head. I raised my arms in front of my face in a defensive gesture.

'So it was you, was it?' he said in a hectoring tone. 'You know you could have killed me?'

He paused. He had apparently just seen my collar. 'Well now, sir,' he said in a more placatory tone, 'even a clergyman shouldn't go round leaving obstacles for people to trip over. Very dangerous.' He stretched out a hand. 'Here, let me help you up.'

I blushed. Keeping my eyes from his and distractedly brushing at my hat, I said, 'I really am very sorry. I fell out of the train and saw my hat roll onto the line. It's new, you know. Are you hurt? I'm very sorry.'

'Never mind, never mind,' he said. 'Teach me to keep my eyes open.' And he continued his walk down the platform.

'What a beginning,' I muttered to myself. I put on the offending hat, picked up my case and moved down the now empty platform. Not many people came to Brimley, it seemed, and they had all gone about their business. My ticket had been taken on the train, so there wasn't even a collector with whom I could try to resume normal human contact.

In the gloom, the station appeared like a large, tiled gents' toilet. It even smelled rather like one. The only ray of warming light came from the ticket office into which the guard had disappeared. I walked past it into the wet cobbled street outside. The station stood above the little town which stretched its dreary panorama before my eyes. To the left, and seemingly just outside the town, the giant winding-wheel of the pit and the huge dead blackened mounds of slag gave clear warning of the nature of the beast. The town itself was dismal in dirty stone. The faded street lamps were reflected already in the slick coating of drizzle, though it was only five o'clock of a September Friday. Behind and to the right of this unwholesome scene the ground rose again into countryside, but even the green of field and tree seemed dirtied.

'Well, here I am,' I said to myself, trying to cheer myself up. I was twenty four, newly ordained, just back from the adulation of my first holiday as a priest. This was my parish, here I was to begin my work. And then a stab of panic ran through me. Where *was* the parish, the church, St Aloysius'? I realized that I had not the faintest idea of which way to turn. It was not the kind of station at which taxis waited in expectation. There was not even another passenger in sight. They had all disappeared around various corners away to their respective homes.

As I hesitated, wondering whether to search out some troglodyte from the deserted station, an ancient Ford car wheezed its way up the cobbled approach to the station entrance, and ground protestingly to a halt. At least I had somebody to ask. Out of the driver's door there emerged the fattest man I had ever seen. He stood about five foot six, and seemed all of that from the straining waistcoat button to the tight stretching of jacket around his spine. Jowls fell from his chin to his chest in unbroken succession. Eyes, black like buttons, bored through layers of flesh. Even his hands were bloated, skin stretched taut like bursting sausages. Below the grotesque belly, two little bandy legs seemed to have withered in the sunless shade cast by that enormous mound.

I gazed down at this apparition with my mouth agape. I forgot even that he was someone of whom I could ask directions. He rolled to a stop in front of me and I recoiled instinctively with the exaggerated motions of the silent films. His head cocked, he looked up at me.

'You'll be the new Father Kennedy,' he said in a voice which combined all the qualities of broken glass and rusty nails. 'You look wet enough behind the ears. Come on lad, I won't eat you. I'm Amos Greenland. When I'm not digging coal out yonder,' he pointed vaguely in the direction of the pit-head, 'I look after things for Father Morrison. A dogsbody, I suppose you'd call me. Welcome to Brimley.'

He poked out his mottled fat hand. I took it limply and felt my bones being ground to powder in his grip. I was to learn later that the same power burnt through every ounce of his round body.

'I'm very glad to meet you, Mr Greenland,' I said, trying to coax blood and life back into my destroyed fingers. 'I was just wondering what to do. I didn't know where the church was or anything.'

'Well I'm here to bring you there,' he replied. 'Old Lizzie here isn't very reliable and I couldn't get her started. Come on then. Is that all the luggage you've got?' His tone implied that he didn't think much to that.

'I sent my books and things on in advance. They may be there already.'

'Well then that's it, isn't it?' he said and lifted my suitcase. The door of the luggage-boot came off in his hands as he threw my poor case into it. 'Don't worry about this,' he said, waving the door around. 'It never comes off when we're going. Climb in then.' He somehow stuck it back on.

I opened the passenger door, wondering whether it too would disconnect itself, but it remained attached to the body of the car. I folded my ungainly form into the cramped space inside. Mr Greenland heaved himself into the driver's seat. The major part of his body was behind me and the wheel seemed embedded in his stomach. But once the car started, there was a delicacy and precision in his handling of the car, which contrasted strangely with his seemingly deformed physique.

We drove steadily through the drenched streets. Rows of back-to-back houses, bleak against the wet cobbles which lay between them, filed off each side of our road. I would, I supposed, come to know them all. Hardly a soul was about, though the warm glow through the curtained windows of the houses gave evidence enough that this seeming ghost town was occupied.

'Come far, have you, Father?' said Amos, breaking the less than comfortable silence. I had been too tongue-tied to venture any conversation.

'Well today I've come only from Kingsmill – that's the other side of York where my parents live. But I got back from a holiday in Ireland only yesterday. So I'm a bit tired.'

I suddenly felt very tired and dispirited. I had never really been alone in my life and I was filled with fear and apprehension about how I would manage in this new strange world.

'You'll be all right with Father Morrison,' vouchsafed Amos. 'He's a good 'un, he won't work you too hard. He doesn't have very good health though, so you'll have to look after him. See he doesn't do too much. He's a beggar for work for himself and he isn't strong enough. Father Mullin, now – he was here before you – he looked after him right. They got on fine.'

My heart sank to my boots again. How would I compare with Father Mullin who looked after him right? I knew so little about what to do, especially about how to look after an ageing and ill parish priest. Amos must have sensed how I felt.

'Don't worry,' he said. 'You'll be fine. You're a strong lad. The people here are very simple and don't expect too much. Miners are very loyal, you know, even if they don't say much. Father Morrison has been here a long time and he understands 'em. He'll keep you right and you'll keep him right.'

A gaunt church with a foreshortened steeple loomed up. I hadn't been noticing which way we had come.

'Here we are,' said Amos cheerfully. 'That's St Aloysius'. Lovely church isn't it?'

It looked absolutely hideous to me. But I was learning. 'Yes, yes,' I said too quickly. 'It looks splendid.'

'And this is the presbytery,' said Amos as we pulled round the back of the church to a solid comfortable two-storey stone house with mullioned windows. Lizzie squealed to what was obviously her normal protesting stop outside the front door. Frosted glass provided half the structure of this large portal and through the glass a welcoming light, fractured into a thousand beams, shone out into what was now a very murky atmosphere.

'It always seems to get dark early here. Must be the coal dust or something I suppose.' Amos seemed entirely unperturbed. He once again wrenched the door of the luggage compartment clear of its fastenings and lifted out my suitcase. He gave a perfunctory ring on a bell set into the stonework and then opened the door and walked into the house. I followed him somewhat timorously, lifting my hat from my head. In a brief moment of survey I saw a pleasantly proportioned carpeted hall from which a polished and beautifully carved wooden staircase led to the upper floor. Four solid and equally polished wooden doors led off from this impressive vestibule.

My gaze was distracted from this first pleasant reconaissance by the simultaneous appearance of three figures. The first was obviously Father Morrison, coming through the door to my right, presumably from his study. The female appearing from the door beyond the staircase at the back of the hall would be the housekeeper. For neither of these did my eyes and attention have more than a second of study. The third figure was a large brindled dog which rushed to a frightening halt straight in front of me, laid back its ears, bared a savage set of fangs, and issued a blood-curdling hissing noise. Terror made me drop my hat. It was having a rough day of it. But this time I made no move to uplift it. If I moved that slavering beast would have me.

'Jasper,' said Father Morrison in a deep commanding voice. 'Get in there, Jasper, and behave yourself.'

The dog shook itself and sidled behind his legs back into the study from which it must have emerged. A final baleful look towards me promised that he looked forward to a future meeting where nobody would be around to stop him tearing my throat out.

'Don't worry about Jasper,' said the priest. 'He's just an old pet and he'll love you when he gets used to you. You must be Father Kennedy. Welcome to St Aloysius'. I'm Father Morrison.'

His hand was warm in mine. He had obviously been a fine figure of a man in his day, as they say in Ireland. Slightly shorter than I, he was broader and more compact. But the years or illness had shrunk the flesh from his bones. His skin had a translucent pallor confirmed by the kindly twinkle of deep blue eyes and the soft cap of fine white hair.

'Very glad to meet you Father.' I stammered, still paralysed by the brindled fury of Jasper. I shook myself and picked up the wretched homburg.

'And this is Miss Nails, our housekeeper.' Father Morrison brought her forward for the introduction.

Miss Nails was small, thin, and acidulous. She gripped my hand with surprising strength and looked me up and down. 'Welcome Father,' she said in a surprisingly deep growl. 'God bless us, you're awful thin. I'll have to fatten you up or Father will be sacking me. I'll make a cup of tea just now, and we'll have supper in about half an hour.'

'Thank you, thank you, Miss Nails.' I was really full of urbane wit.

'Amos,' said Father Morrison, 'take Father Kennedy up to his room and show him where everything is, and then come on down and we'll all have a cup of tea.'

Amos had been standing as immovable as one of the pyramids through these brief introductions. 'Come on lad,' he said and rolled his way up the carved staircase. Dumping my suitcase outside a door at the top which led into the room immediately above Father Morrison's, he opened the door and said, 'That's your bed-sitter.'

And pointing in the manner of a world-weary courier, 'That's the bathroom, the lavatory, Father Morrison's bedroom. There you are now. I'll just let you freshen up. Then come on down and join us and old Sadie will begin the fattening-up. Father Mullin put on two stones while he was here so there's hope for you yet. But,' and he patted his massive belly, 'it's only beer will put that on you.' He charted his way happily down the stairs.

I looked into the bathroom and lavatory which were the same as bathrooms and lavatories everywhere. I did notice how immaculately clean they were. Further tribute to the redoubtable Miss Nails Would I ever graduate to calling her Sadie?

I moved across the landing, switched on the light in the room that was to be mine and closed the door on my new kingdom. The boxes I had sent in advance were neatly stacked near the wardrobe. My offending and offended hat I threw on the bed and then I sank with relief into the comfortable armchair pulled up to the glowing warmth of the coal fire. I had come home.

A moving shape slid from under the bed and there standing before my horrified eyes was Jasper. His large head was on a level with my own, his menacing brown eyes fixed unflinchingly on my throat. I dared neither stand nor move. I had time to issue only one terrified yelp before his mouth opened and a long red and surprisingly soft tongue licked my hand. The sweat was running off me.

'Good Jasper, good dog,' I whimpered and ventured my

other hand to pat his ugly head. With a cat-like moan he snuggled into me, burying his head between my legs.

'Good Jasper, good dog,' I repeated, relief flooding through me. But I still dare not move. Finally in desperation I struggled to my feet at which his mouth fastened with a kindly gentleness around my wrist. It was in that unlikely condition that I reappeared at Father Morrison's door.

'Ah Father Kennedy,' said he rising. 'I see you've made friends with Jasper. A grand old beast he is. He'll love you for life now.' My face must have revealed the remnants of my terror and both he and Amos burst into delighted howls of laughter.

'Welcome again boy,' said Father Morrison between his whoops. 'You're home now in St Aloysius'.'

## CHAPTER TWO

I HAD arrived on a Friday, so with palpitations of fear I faced the weekend duties. As I sat gingerly for the first time in a confessional box I imagined all the insoluble problems that would be thrust upon me. But the relief I felt when I came out of the box was more the beginning of appreciation that the people who confessed were weak humans like myself, and not examiners of my knowledge of theology. I was nonetheless startled when a little old woman, seated in one of the benches, shouted at me as I passed her.

'You're the new priest aren't you?' she roared. 'You'll have to speak up you know. I'm deaf and I can't hear you. What did you say my penance was? I've said a whole rosary. Will that do?'

Rather than compete in this shouting match, I nodded vigorously and gave her what I hoped was a reassuring and saintly smile. To my horror she leaned across, grabbed my hand in clawlike fingers and planted a very wet kiss on it.

'Ha!' I yelped. 'Well yes . . . thank you very much.' I could feel the blush rising from my neck.

'What did you say, love?' She cocked her ear at me.

'Thank you very much.'

The two other people in the church turned in some alarm at my wild bellow. I smiled grotesquely again, freed my hand from hers and made my way through the sacristy into the house.

'I see you've met Nellie. Nellie Ryan,' smiled Father Morrison. 'She's a great old stick, but deaf as a post. Sixty something she is, and still loves to go round to the "Black Bull" with her jug and get her beer every night. She's in your district so you'll keep meeting her. You just have to shout back at her.'

'I was surprised when she grabbed my hand, Father. I

didn't know what she was doing or what I should do. I'll get used to it, Father; it's all rather strange at first.'

'Of course you will,' said Father Morrison. 'Come on now, you'll be ready for your supper.'

'Too thin,' growled Miss Nails, as she carried in the food. 'You're far too thin, Father. I don't want the pair of you sick on me, so eat up.' She bustled out.

Father Morrison seemed almost embarrassed. 'She's an old fuss-pot,' he said too heartily. 'I sometimes don't keep the best of health but nothing to worry about.'

Since he was to eat nothing but a lightly boiled egg, while I tucked into bacon, sausage and chips, I wasn't too reassured. Old Amos, I remembered, had also said that Father Morrison wasn't well. But I didn't know him well enough, nor was I sure enough of myself to pursue the matter further.

On Sunday I was to say the two early Masses, read the notices and preach. As I moved from the altar to the pulpit nervousness flooded over me again. To make things worse I tripped over my long vestments as I mounted the steps of the pulpit, and arrived in that exalted spot on my knees and with my glasses round my mouth.

'This is the twelfth Sunday after Pentecost,' I squeaked. Switching my eyes briefly from the back wall of the church at which I was fixedly gazing, I saw smiles and nudges among he parishioners seated below me. 'This is the twelfth Sunday after Pentecost,' I repeated in a deep bass voice, concluding with an involuntary and high pitched 'Ha!'

This was obviously the best turn the parishioners had seen since the old music-halls. Blushing and sweating, my glasses misting up with the heat I was generating, I somehow stumbled through the unfamiliar routine. My sermon was a disaster. Half way through I completely lost my train of thought and with numbing abruptness blessed them and galloped from the pulpit. Even I could hear the quiet buzz of the congregation. They had been landed with a right loony.

The second Mass was better. I had learned from the ghastliness of the first. I held up my vestments as I mounted the pulpit steps. My glasses did not steam up. The notices were read in what seemed to me a normal tone of voice. But the sermon! Again, and at the same point I went blank. Not an idea. After seconds or minutes of total silence I said, 'Do forgive me. My mind has just closed. Come back next week and I'll do better.'

This time there was almost applause as I moved unhurriedly back to the altar.

'I'm learning!' I thought. 'I'll never be as bad as that again.'

But as Father Morrison took me during the week on a guided tour of the parish I had to bear a good deal of kindly raillery. Amos Greenland, inevitably, led the charge.

'Right comedian you've got there,' he said to Father Morrison as we walked into the miner's cottage, which seemed to strain at the seams just to accommodate Amos' bulk.

'Now, now,' said Father Morrison, 'he did very well. How would you like it, standing up there for the first time in front of hundreds of people? Anyway it's surely better to make them laugh than to bore them to tears?'

'It is that,' growled Amos. 'I'm normally never awake enough to be able to remember what the priest says. But Sunday! I remember every word.' And as he almost exploded with laughter he clapped me on the shoulder numbing my whole left side.

'You'll do lad. I'll look forward to Sunday now.'

'Where's Agnes?' said Father Morrison changing the subject, to my great relief.

'She's just down at t'shop Father,' replied Amos. 'She be back in a tick to make you a cup of tea.'

And as Father Morrison started to protest he said 'Now just you sit down there. I know you've been taking Father Kennedy round all week, and it's too much for you. So sit down and rest a minute. He's got years to find all the places and see all the people. But you won't have years if you go on like this.'

Amos beckoned to an armchair and then sat down himself. He seemed embarrassed by such a long speech. 'How are you liking Brimley anyway?' he asked me, dismissing any argument. As I paused to make a suitably approving reply, 'You'll have to get rid of that hat, you know,' he said, pointing to the homburg sitting primly on my knee. 'Makes you look like a boy dressing up as a man. Not even Father Morrison wears a hat like that.'

His laughter took away any hurt. I looked wryly down at the hat which was only a month old. Well, it would have to go, I resolved; homburgs and Brimley didn't mix.

At this point the door opened and a very small handsome woman, neat to the point of perfection, gloved hands holding a shopping basket, walked in.

'Hallo Agnes.' Father Morrison rose from his chair. 'This, believe it or not,' he said to me, 'is Mrs Greenland. Agnes, this is Father Kennedy, our new curate.'

'Very pleased to meet you Father,' she said, taking my hand. 'Don't let that big blusterer of a husband of mine bully you. I've got him right under my thumb, so if you've any trouble, just come to me.'

She smiled affectionately at Amos who looked positively coy. For the first time I witnessed the fullness and content of a happy marriage. With some alarm I felt a twinge of envy of the warmth and understanding that was so clearly shared by this unlikely couple. The cup of tea which Agnes produced with the minimum of fuss and maximum of efficiency tasted better, or so it seemed to me, just because it was a product of such secure affection.

'What a very happy couple,' I commented to Father Morrison as we walked the last leg back to the presbytery. 'Do they have any children?'

'It's a great sorrow to them both,' said Father Morrison. 'Perhaps that's why Amos is so good to us. We're his children I suppose.'

But the homes of Brimley were not all so full of tranquillity. Even in that first week I could see some of the grinding poverty, the domestic discords, the unhappy and resentful children, which made Brimley a small cross-section of humanity. As well as the troubling envy of the Greenlands' happiness, I felt anger, pity, hopelessness at the plight of so many others. Physical suffering, too, I began to see was no stranger to this place. It was a fact of life to mining communities, borne with the same grim patience as the danger, dirt and discomfort which their work demanded. I was learning – not just how to compose myself in a pulpit – but about real people, real problems, so far removed from the sanitized, academic discussions of the Seminary.

'I must take you to meet Dr Murphy before I let you loose on your own. He's our doctor.' Father Morrison had been patient, indefatigable through what seemed a very long week. 'He and his wife are rather odd. You'll see. Irish of course. Don't be surprised at anything. I think you should find the visit intriguing.' He twinkled as he said this. And he repeated the warning as we walked up the drive to the square-built stone mansion that was the doctor's home and surgery. 'Don't look surprised at anything.'

Somewhat apprehensively, then, I followed him through the imposing front door which a tall formidable-looking woman had opened to our ring.

'I've brought the new curate, Father Kennedy, to see yourself and the doctor,' said Father Morrison.

A pair of warm soft hands enfolded my outstretched palm.

'So good of you to come Father. It's lovely to see you.'

The warm gentle brogue purred from this big woman. Blonde, blue-eyed and imposingly fleshed, Mrs Murphy looked like a Nordic goddess. Releasing my hand, she moved like a ship in sail towards the room on the right of the airy, chequered hall.

'Tom's in here having a wee snooze before evening surgery.'

We followed her into the high-ceilinged, light, warm and welcoming room. Slumped in a chair near the cheerful fire, a gentle snore wobbling his lips, lay Dr Murphy. A mane of blue-black hair crowned a face angular even in repose. A very impressive looking couple, I thought. His wife's hand on his shoulder brought him awake with a jerk.

'Wha . . . what,' he mouthed, his eyes wide in an empty stare. 'Oh, hallo there Father. Sorry. Just having a little sleep.'

'This is Father Kennedy, Tom,' purred Mrs Murphy. 'Isn't it nice of himself and Father Morrison to come up?'

'I've heard about you, Father,' said Dr Murphy, now on his feet and shaking himself. 'You're welcome. Cead mile Failte, as they say in God's own country. You're a bit of a comedian I hear.' His eyes wrinkled into a smile. 'Well now. Let's have a drink on that. A drop of whisky for you Father Morrison? And what'll you have, young man? I've an Irish whisky here that would bring the dead back to life.'

'I don't really drink, Doctor,' I said uncomfortably – everyone seemed so at ease compared to me – 'but I'll take a drop of your Irish since you recommend it.'

'Good, good,' he effused. 'Sit down then. You'll get varicose veins standing about like that. Usual gin for you, Maeve?' he said to his wife.

'Lovely,' she breathed. She seemed always to speak in a tone of wonderment or excitement. 'I'll get some ice for us all.'

As she moved majestically out of the room, the doctor carried his gangling frame down to a beautifully carved bureau in the window alcove. Bottles and glasses, produced with a flourish, were manipulated with an expertise bred of long practice. Lady Maeve reappeared with the ice in a small silver bucket and an equally fine silver jug of water. The drinks dispensed, we sat under the beaming approval of Mrs Murphy. The usual chat about how I was enjoying Brimley followed. It was a ritual with which I was now familiar.

'And how are you keeping, Father?' said Dr Murphy to Father Morrison.

Before he could reply, Mrs Murphy rose in commanding majesty. 'Look Tom,' she said. 'I'll take Father Kennedy away, and you can have a talk with Father Morrison. Naughty Father, you haven't had a check-up for a long time, and you know you should. Come on now Father,' silencing Father Morrison with an elegant arm. 'I'll take care of you. Come on.'

Unfortunately I was just taking the first sip of my whisky and whether it went down the wrong way, or was just so strong that it nearly took the enamel off my teeth, I choked on it. A paroxysm of coughing followed as I spluttered my way in the wake of the receding Mrs Murphy. Across the hall into the room on the other side she led me, a room as light and pastel-elegant as the one we had left. I sat in some embarrassment, my face purple, my eyes streaming.

'Ah, don't worry about a thing,' she said. 'Just take your time and you'll be all right.'

'I'm very sorry, Mrs Murphy. I think I'm just not used to drinking. I do apologise.'

'Don't be foolish,' she chided me. 'And you're to call me Maeve. I think we're going to get on very well together.'

I sat down on a couch, carefully placing my whisky on the little table by its side. As I straightened up I felt the warmth of a rounded haunch, pressing softly against my leg.

'Ha!' I screeched. I must have risen nearly a foot from the couch.

'There, there, Father,' soothed Mrs Murphy. 'It always takes a few minutes when your drink has gone the wrong way.' Her hand smoothed my trouser leg. I felt in imminent danger of a seizure.

But Mrs Murphy, Maeve, moved not an inch from me on the couch. Her hand still on my leg, her eyes round and rapturously fixed on mine, she sighed rather than spoke.

'Now Father, I know how hard it is for you young priests. You've no one to talk to, no one to share your problems with. So any time you're lonely, any time you want a bit of comfort, you just come on up here. Tom's out most of the day on his doctoring, so I'm nearly always here on my own. Won't that be nice?'

I sat transfixed, my mouth opening and closing like a landed fish. 'Hargh,' I gurgled. 'That's wonderful, most kind of you. Don't you think we'd better be going back in to Father Morrison? We have to go soon. Tea you know.'

And I rose, as if shot from a cannon, nearly displacing Mrs Murphy from her seat. 'Ha!' I repeated. 'Let's go through then.' I set off as though anxious to qualify for the Olympic hundred metres.

'That's fine, then,' said Mrs Murphy. 'I'll expect you very soon and we can find out all about each other.'

In spite of my haste, she moved smoothly past to open the door for me. Father Morrison and the Doctor were emerging from the room across the hall. I heard just the final snatch of their talk.

'I'll be round to see you early next week,' Dr Murphy was saying. 'And you just take those pills and let's see if they improve things at all.'

'Thanks, thanks Tom,' said Father Morrison almost irritably, and cutting short any further revelations. 'Come on now Father, Sadie will give us a spanking if we're not home on time. Thanks for everything Tom – and you Maeve. See you both again soon.'

He almost rushed out the front door.

'I told you they were an odd pair,' smiled Father Morrison as we walked home. 'How did you get on with Maeve?' he chuckled. I blushed. 'I thought so,' said Father Morrison. 'She's a terrible woman but don't take her seriously. I think if you really gave her a bit of a squeeze and looked as though you meant it she'd be as frightened as you. She's just a big soft kindly lump with nymphomaniac tendencies.' He positively barked with laughter. 'And Tom's almost an alcoholic. We saw him at his best today, but normally he's half-cut. One of these days somebody's going to report him. But he's so good with the people here, that most of them don't mind at all.'

'He seemed worried enough about you, Father,' I said.

'Ha, bosh,' he snorted. 'Just a wee bit of the blood pressure. Nothing to worry about.' He dismissed the subject.

I woke in the night after a dream in which Maeve Murphy was sinuously undressing before me. I would have to be very careful to keep her soft charms away from me.

# CHAPTER THREE

THE long nights seemed to close in rapidly. The keen sting of frost sharpened the edges of Brimley, and made more cosy the warm rooms into which my visiting took me. But in these early days I was still unsure of many of the addresses in my little book, and I found myself in many an odd situation as a result.

I was looking for Nellie – Nellie Ryan the deaf old lady who had so startled me that first night when she had kissed my hand. Father Morrison had filled me in with further background on Nellie. She was a widow whose husband had been killed during those odd pre-war days when the I.R.A. had mounted their unprofitable bombing attacks on targets in England. A bomb he had been carrying to some target had exploded, leaving Jim Ryan, patriot, a mess of miscellaneous pieces scraped from the fortunately empty street where he was walking.

Nellie had mourned him though she had no sympathy with his aims or methods. But the grim thirties had curtailed her sorrow. The harsh fight for survival for herself and her five children had led her by some mysterious route to Brimley. Even now in more prosperous days and with her children all off her hands and strewn around the country, she continued to char – to clean houses, wash clothes. If I could overcome the barrier of her deafness, I was looking forward to a chat with Nellie. She was above loneliness, said Father Morrison, always cheerful, bright and good.

She lived in what was called in Brimley, a 'Yard', a little cul-de-sac in which four or five small houses burrowed together, as if in secret. The street outside had the widely spaced gas lamps which still passed for street lighting in Brimley. The Yard's impenetrable darkness was lessened only slightly by the thin glow from the downstairs windows of the houses. Which was Nellie's, I wondered. I had her number, but none of the doors seemed to sport such mundane identification.

Taking my courage in both hands I knocked at the first door whose adjoining window glimmered into the darkness. The door burst open, and framed in the dim glow that slanted from the room stood the most enormous man I had ever seen. What his face, or even his clothes were like, it was impossible to discern in that half light.

'Come on in then,' he growled taking me by the arm before I could even open my mouth. 'It's too cold out there. Come inside.'

I had little choice as he propelled me into his den. A fire crackling in the grate was the only note of cheer. No carpet. A couple of rickety chairs round a card table, and an extremely dirty, sagging armchair were the only furnishings. Two plates, a packet of salt and a huge mug sat on the card table, outlined against what appeared to be two sections of a grimy bedspread now serving as curtains. They had appeared quite inviting from outside.

'I can't pay you this week.' A rather diffident and embarrassed grunt this time. 'I've been on the sick and haven't even collected my Lloyd George yet.'

I had been long enough in Brimley to know that in their quaint vocabulary that ancient leader of the Liberal Party still stood for unemployment money. But I had no idea what the poor man meant. I looked at his massive figure. He must be a miner – everyone in Brimley was a miner. But how did he squeeze that enormous carcase along the narrow channels that still passed for roadways down the mine? His face was broad and Indian-looking, full of flat planes chiselled as though from a rock.

'I'm very sorry. I'm looking for Nellie, Mrs Ryan.'

'Aren't you the rent man? I thought you were t'rent man. Who are you if you're not the rent man? He always comes at this time.'

I realized that my coat collar was up around my ears to protect me from the sharp night air. I pulled it down revealing my collar. 'I'm Father Kennedy,' I stumbled. 'I'm new here up at St Aloysius'. And I was looking for Nellie Ryan, Mrs Ryan.'

'Why didn't you bloody say so? I can't do with your lot, never could. I'm Matt McGinley and I'm a communist. How do you like that?' There was an air of triumph about his pronouncement as though he had outwitted me in some major confrontation.

'Well, that's very nice, I'm sure,' I said, somewhat ineffectually. 'But I'm looking for Nellie Ryan. She does live here in the Yard doesn't she? Or have I got the wrong Yard?'

'Aye, she lives here,' said the enormous Mr McGinley staring at me. 'Next door. But sit down while you're 'ere. You'll never get in this bloody house again, so you may as well make t'most of it. You're always wanting to "convert" people you lot. Go on then, convert me.'

A bellow of challenging laughter followed this demand. Nonplussed and quite out of my depth, I sat gingerly on one of the chairs near the card table. Communism had been discussed in the Seminary, but its neat theories seemed a world away from this hulking lout, the first real-life communist I had ever met.

'Have a drink.'

It was an order, not a request. He moved to the cupboard in the wall near the fireplace. A bottle of beer was almost swallowed in one hand as he slapped two dirty looking mugs down on the card table. 'Always talk better with a glass o' beer in me hand.' He poured rapidly and pushed one foaming mug in my direction. 'I were brought up a Catholic. My mother, God rest her, spent all her life in that bloody church of yours. She used to even make me go. But when it were needed there were no help from God, or church. She died at fifty of cancer, screaming in pain. Where were your loving God then eh?'

I sipped my beer slowly, pondering my reply. Emotional debate was not my strong point. But Mr McGinley, after a venomous gulp of his own beer, burst on with his tirade.

'Now t' communists don't make promises they can't keep. I don't give ought for all their hogwash about t' proletariat and dialectic or whatever it is, but at least they do work for ordinary people. And they have improved things. It's them and not the Labour Party who's responsible for our better conditions in the mines. We're not fully there yet, but by God, things is very different from when I first went down. So you'll have to promise and deliver a hell of a lot if you're going to get people like me to church. What has the Church ever done for us?'

Echoes of the large lady on the railway platform with her 'What's the Church going to do about that?' filled my head. To quote the theology textbooks about grace and salvation seemed inappropriate as a reply to the heat and passion of Mr McGinley's feelings.

'Perhaps if you could see your mother now, she'd be able to put things in a different order of importance.' At least he was listening to me. 'I don't know why God allowed your mother to suffer such agony, but I'm sure He knows, and she knows now, too. Suffering and pain seem to be a part of life. We can lessen them – as they've done in the mines, but they can never take them away. I think your communists, without realizing it, are doing exactly the same as the Church tries to do. But the Church knows it will never be completely successful, while the communists think they will. Are they going to stop people dying of cancer?'

That was just about the longest speech I had ever made. It seemed to have stopped even the formidable Mr McGinley in his tracks. I took another sip of my beer.

'Aye well,' grunted the immobile giant. 'That's as good an answer as ever I've had. I like that. Somebody who stands up for themselves. I'm not saying I'm convinced mind, but I always respect somebody who isn't afraid to speak out. You can come again,' he concluded to my great surprise. 'Would you like another beer?' There was almost humility in the request.

'No, no thank you,' I said. 'I really must go to Mrs Ryan. But I will come back if you want me to. I enjoyed our talk.'

I had too, even though I was petrified most of the time. If you start an encounter thinking you might end it with a broken jaw, then anything less than that can only be good.

And I had the bonus of a mug of good beer. I counted my blessings.

'I'll go and see Mrs Ryan now. Next door you say? Could you show me which side?'

The monster lumbered to the door. 'You'll have to knock very hard. She's very deaf you know. Here, I'll take you in.'

He moved through his own doorway and beat on the immediately adjoining door to his right as though he were trying to cave it in. He then turned the handle and beckoned me like some conspirator to follow him.

'It's the Father, Nellie,' he roared and must have been heard at the church, a mile away. 'He's come to see you.'

Nellie was sitting cosily by the fire. Draped in a shawl, she was knitting some hideous looking garment. The contrast between the comfortable neatness of her little domain, and that of Matt, her neighbour, was dramatic.

'What do you mean barging in here, Matt McGinley?' she shouted at him. 'Don't you even knock when you go into somebody else's house?'

He moved towards her with what appeared to be some caution. He bent towards her ear and opened his lungs again. 'I did knock Nellie. And it's the Father.' He gestured towards me. 'He's come to see you, you old Irish goat. I just brought him in. So stop getting ratty at me.'

As Nellie moved to peer round his great body, he jumped back in apprehension, seemingly fearing a blow.

'Hallo Father,' said Nellie. 'Sorry I didn't see you. What on earth are you doing with this big ape? He hasn't been to church in years. Should be ashamed of himself, so he should.' She turned towards Matt, who again jumped as if he'd been shot.

'Now now Nellie,' he said. 'Don't do anything foolish. The Father came to my door by mistake, so I was doing you a favour by bringing him round. He's strange here you know. Aren't you Father?' There was a pleading in his voice, which was becoming hoarse now from the continuous shouting. He appeared even to have shrunk in the storm of Nellie's abuse.

'That's right Nellie, Mrs Ryan.' I was screaming myself.

'He's been a great help. Thank you very much Mr McGinley, I'll come again.'

He scuttled out, touching his head with what appeared to be a gesture of reverence as he did so. The door slammed, shaking the house.

'Has he closed the door?' said Nellie, for whom obviously the crack of doom would pass unnoticed. 'He's a silly big lump you know, Father. But he's as soft as putty really. Anyway come and sit down and let me look at you.'

Her sharp warm eyes gazed at me as I sat at the other side of the hearth. We were reflected in each other's glasses as we played this odd visual game.

'How are you Mrs Ryan?' A scintillating opening gambit.

'What did you say?' said Nellie. 'I'm a bit deaf you know, you'll have to talk up to me. Why don't you just sit there and I'll do the talking. I know what you'll be asking anyway, and it saves you shouting.'

This extraordinary but very sensible proposition was so appropriate to the situation that I could only nod in agreement. Here was no whining old lady lamenting her loss of hearing, but a practical sharp intelligence determined to make the best of a wayward world and not complain.

'I suppose you've heard from Father Morrison about my poor, silly, wild James? I pray for him every day, asking the good Lord to understand him as well as I did. There wasn't an ounce of malice in the poor eejut you know Father. He hated the English but not personally, and he'd never willingly hurt one of them. He'd have been going to blow up a Post Office or a bank or something that night. He never spoke to me about it, of course, but it would be a building or something he was after, not people. Even when he did kill anybody by accident, it was only his poor self. God rest him anyway. I miss him. It's lonely without a man in the house, especially when you have young children. Have you ever noticed how many Irish people can't have children, Father? And we're all supposed to have such big families according to the stories.' Her eyes twinkled at me. A very well adjusted lady was Nellie. 'Aren't you Irish yourself Father?' she asked.

I nodded. 'But I was born in England, Nellie, so I've got the best or the worst of both worlds. My father was like your James in some ways, even though he never did anything about it. But he taught me to love Ireland even though I was English. It's a bit of a drawback in some ways.'

Nellie nodded, though I wasn't at all sure that she'd heard me. 'When you get to my age, Father, you'll know it doesn't really matter. Just loving people is all that really counts. Take that big lump next door. He was goodness itself to my children when Jim went, though he pretended not to be. He was the only son of his mother and his father was killed in the pit. When she died he was a lost soul. He blamed the Church for it.' She snorted. 'But all the time in the midst of his own sorrow he acted like a father to my children and whenever they come back, they're in to see him almost before they come in here. He seems to like you, though he'd have nothing to do with any of the others, even Father Morrison. So you stick with him and maybe you'll get him back. Anyway it'll be a good excuse for you to come here often too. I'm always glad to see somebody. Takes my mind off this silly knitting. Do you know what this is then? It's a sweater for that big tub next door. If I didn't look after him some way, he'd let everything go. Silly man.' Suddenly she rolled the knitting into a bundle and stood herself up. 'Now you'll be having a cup of tea. I always do myself at this time.'

No answer was possible as Nellie shuffled into the kitchen part of her cosy room. If I couldn't make her hear when I was shouting at her face, there was no way she was going to tune into me as she moved away. In any case, though I had done very little talking, my own throat was beginning to feel hoarse.

When we finally stood up from the tea and more of Nellie's observant but kindly comments about various of the parishioners, I felt exhausted. It was time anyway to be returning to the presbytery for supper, or I would have to face the wrath of Miss Nails. Again Neilie took my hand in her withered and calloused grip. Again she lowered her head and reverently kissed my hand. I stroked her grey hair affectionately and went again into the night.

Nellie and Matt. If all the parisioners had as much humanity about them as these two, life was going to be exhausting but rewarding. I smiled to myself, and walked straight into a lamp post.

# CHAPTER FOUR

ONE Friday morning after I had been a month or so in St Aloysius', Father Morrison breezed into the school. He had dropped by earlier in the week, of course, so his visit now was no surprise. Sister Clare greeted him as though he were the Messiah new-born.

'Good morning Father,' she intoned, her reverential bow taking her halfway to the floor. 'Good morning Father,' to me.

'Good morning Fathers,' chorused the forty children in her class, galvanized into action by a frenzied waving from Sister Clare, who also mouthed the words to them, lest they forget this chant.

The school was the usual old-fashioned stone building with high ceilings and long narrow windows, pointed at the top, in what had been considered ecclesiastical style in the late nineteenth century. A shaft of sudden sunlight bathed our high room with its green-painted roof joists. Father Morrison could hardly have hoped for this mystical aura to add to his presence.

'Good morning Sister,' he said in a kind of half-chant of his own. 'Good morning children.' And he paused. 'What are we going to do today?' he asked in his sing-song official voice.

Hands shot into the air like a graveside presenting of arms.

'Yes Willie?' said Father Morrison, pointing to a tow-haired freckled cherub, chunks of whose unwashed torso peered through holes in his ragged jumper.

'We're going to play football?' There was an aching note of hope in his voice.

'Miss, Miss, Sister, Sister,' hissed the smugly superior rest of them who knew. And even 'Father, Father,' from the most superior of all, Jennifer. Jennifer's pleated pinafore dress in some violent tartan and her snowy white blouse exuded saintly and clean certainty.

'Yes, Jennifer,' encouraged Father Morrison, now on a winner, and ignoring poor Willie.

'Please Father, we're going to Confession,' she breathed. Nobody had ever spoken of the Holy Grail or Camelot with such ecstasy. She smiled and fluttered her eyes. She would be quite a girl some day and it wouldn't be when talking about Confession.

'That's right,' beamed Father Morrison. 'We're going to Confession. Now remember when you come into Church with Sister, be thinking of all the bad things you've done since your last Confession. And ask God to help you to be sorry for them so that you'll never, never do them again. And when Father Kennedy and myself have heard your confession, go out of the box, kneel down and say your penance carefully, and then wait for Sister to bring you all back here.' He paused again. He was a great one for the dramatic pause. 'What's a penance, anyway?' he asked.

This time the hands went up tentatively. That was a killer of a question. But Willie, never learning, had his hand waving like a demented railway signal.

'Miss, Miss,' he pleaded, ignoring the Fatherhood of Father Morrison and the Sisterhood of Sister Clare. 'Miss, Miss,' with all the yearning of a soul in agony.

Against his better judgment, but because he was at heart a kindly man and wanted to put Willie out of is misery, Father Morrison nodded to Willie. 'Yes Willie,' he said with some trepidation.

'It's a kind of ship, Miss,' said Willie. He'd done a little project on ships recently and he had come across a pinnace. It was near enough and the fact that it seemed to have nothing to do with Confession was no problem to Willie. Nothing he ever did in school seemed to have any connection with anything else, or with life at all. 'A small ship, Miss,' he said desperately as the expected rounds of applause failed to materialize.

Father Morrison, who hadn't done a project on ships, had no idea what the little toe-rag had in mind. His own mind went completely blank. He had asked for bread and been given a stone.

Sister Clare, who was more used to Willie than was Father Morrison, and who was a kindly soul herself, quickly got the situation in hand. 'Now Willie, Father's talking about Confession, not the sea. But it was a good try.' She smiled at Willie to lessen his permanent burden of being wrong. 'So children come on. Every time you go to Confession, Father – both Fathers,' turning to include me in the act, 'ask you to say some prayers as a penance after they have forgiven your sins. So why do they do that? As Father said, what is a penance?'

Hands went up more surely now, and Sister, obviously knowing her flock and wishing to avoid any further blows to Father's pride, picked a little girl. Not Jennifer, but Jennifer-ish. The wee child blushed happily and said all in a rush, 'Please Sister, it's something we do to make up for the bad things we've done.'

'Splendid!' roared Father Morrison. 'That's the idea, isn't it. You see now what it is?' he asked Willie whose aggrieved face still indicated that a ship was a much better bet.

'Yes, Miss,' sulked Willie, convinced neither of Father Morrison's virility nor the superiority of prayers over ships.

'Good then,' said Father Morrison. 'Let's go on into the church now and we'll all go to Confession.'

At least he tried, I thought. Nobody ever tried to put us at ease when I was small. It was just into the forbidding gloom of the church, and in rapid order, into the even more confined darkness of the confessional. Perhaps these poor children were going through the same misery as had been my lot, wondering in terror if they'd forgotten any sin.

In the church I sat myself comfortably on the padded chair on my side of the confessional box. I pulled the thin strip of purple which stood in for more elaborate vestments around my neck, adjusted my glasses and pushed my ear near to the grille which linked my side of the box to the other. There seemed few fears or hesitancies among the children as they trooped in one after the other.

'Bless me Father for I have sinned,' sang each in an unreal monotone. 'It is four weeks since my last Confession. I have been disobedient ten times, told lies twice, fought with my brothers and sisters six times, used bad words three times.'

I was amazed at the supposed accuracy of their numbering. A few confessed that they had missed Mass, but the majority parroted their little rhyme without fear or feeling. I gave them all three Hail Marys to say for their penance, and as I intoned the words of Absolution they said their Act of Contrition in the same unearthly and I'm sure meaningless tone.

'Oh my God, because thou art so good I am very sorry that I have sinned against thee, and I will not sin again.' Invariably the last few words were said as they burst through the door into the freedom of the church outside.

Finally one child made a dramatic entrance. He, his masculinity audible in his first words, fell through the door, noisily banging what must have been his head on the partition between us. I thought he was coming through.

'Bloody and damn,' he said very distinctly. An appropriate if slightly ungrammatical comment. It was Willie. I recognized the voice.

When he had scrambled from the floor, breathing and sighing heavily, and deposited himself on the kneeler, he knocked at the grille.

'Are you there, Father?' he shouted as though I had somehow dematerialized.

'Yes, yes, I'm here,' I replied, choking back the 'Willie.' It wouldn't do to let him know that I knew who he was.

'Oh,' said Willie, still in a raucous bellow. 'Bless me Father for I have sinned. It is so many weeks since my last Confession.'

'So many,' not any number. I let it pass.

'I have swore so many times.' Willie obviously had no time for numerical accuracy. He'd been told to say 'so many', so 'so many' it was. As he continued with the rhythmic chant his voice rose. He cut out completely in the middle of one of his 'so manys'.

'Yes,' I said encouragingly.

A terrible shriek erupted from poor Willie. 'Please Father, I'm going to commit adultery.' And with despair in every syllable, 'I have committed adultery.'

My glasses nearly fell off my nose. I just couldn't picture

Willie with some married matron, and especially not in the confessional. And then above his laments another sound impinged through the grille. A steady trickle. Willie was wetting his pants. At least in my inexperience I had enough presence of mind to try to calm him. I coughed in some embarrassment.

'That's alright Willie. Don't worry. Just say three Hail Marys and your Act of Contrition.'

Never have the words of sorrow been so quickly mouthed and even at that he wasn't halfway through before rushing out of the door. My own words of Absolution I projected after his flying figure.

Nobody followed him in. He was the last. I waited until I heard Sister marshall them out of the church back to the school before I came out. I looked into the other side. There in a sad little pool was the evidence of Willie's adultery.

In the sacristy were cloths used by the cleaning ladies. I removed Willie's adultery and sprayed a little air freshener.

'I try to get one class in for Confession every Friday,' said Father Morrison as we walked back into the presbytery. 'Very good for them you know. Gets them into the habit of regular Confession. Their parents would never send a lot of them otherwise.'

I made no comment on the lack of logic. Their parents presumably had had the same treatment and much good it had done many of them. I made no comment either on Willie's adultery. That would have been breaking the seal of the confessional, by which we were bound to preserve secrecy about whatever we heard. I suppose that a trickle of wee counted. Poor Willie.

# CHAPTER FIVE

FATHER MORRISON was the Dean of our local Conference. This simply meant he was the Chairman of the local parishes whenever they met, as they did about once a month during the winter. And of course he had to host the first Conference. The meeting, which seemed to be less important than the rest of the proceedings, took place in the late morning, and was followed by a jovial lunch and an afternoon of togetherness. This I was to discover meant cards and drink.

Sadie, as I had now begun to call her, was in endless debate with Father Morrison as to what to serve for the meal. The housekeepers vied with each other to provide the best meal, but I was quite sure that none would outdo Sadie.

The day before the Conference, I sat as usual in Sadie's pleasant kitchen. 'Have you decided what the feast will be tomorrow?' I asked.

'Never you mind, Father. Just leave it all to me and I guarantee you won't be disappointed.'

The twinkle in her eye removed any sense of rebuke. Nonetheless I affected to be monstrously hurt.

'I see, Sadie. I'm just the curate and not fit to be told anything. Ah well, I know my place.'

'Now don't you be so silly,' said Sadie, adding, 'Father,' almost as an afterthought. 'I was only joking. There's no secret at all.' She blushed, I declare.

'Sorry, Sadie. I was joking too. I'm just a nosey young brat.'

'Well,' and she paused impressively. 'We're starting with smoked salmon. I have a cousin who's a fisherman and he always sends me half a salmon he's caught, smoked by one of his friends. In Scotland you know, they have the best salmon, and the best smokers. Then I'm giving them – you too, of course – a homemade soup, potato and leek. And for the main course I'm roasting a lovely piece of beef, sirloin on the bone, and just you watch how Father Morrison carves it. The man's a genius with a carving knife. And there will be several sweets of course, and cheese, biscuits and coffee.'

I was taken aback at this recital of gastronomic delights. Not that I had any doubts about Sadie's abilities. But I had not anticipated such a feast. My astonishment must have registered on my face.

'You look surprised, Father. We have only the one Conference every year. It's like a birthday party. So you wouldn't expect me to give them just a chop or something would you? Father deals with the wine and the rest of the drinks. You'll have to help him serve them, so you'd better have a word with him.'

I had given very little thought to the Conference before this. It would be an occasion for meeting many of my fellow priests, but beyond that I had considered it not at all. Now it loomed as a great occasion, and nervousness at the unknown flooded through me.

Sadie, with her usual kindly observation hastened to reassure me. 'Don't be worried, Father. You'll enjoy it. Everybody has a lovely time. You'll see. Just relax, and you'll see what a happy day it will be. So come on now, clear out of my kitchen and let me get on with the preparations.'

She drew herself up to er full thin five feet and tried to loom over my gangling frame as I lounged in a chair. I sprang to my feet in mock alarm and spoilt the whole scene by side-swiping a jug off the table. Fortunately it was metal, but my confusion was no less than if I had scattered shards of precious porcelain over the kitchen floor. 'Sorry Sadie,' I flustered. 'I'm a clumsy idiot.'

'Never mind, Father – no harm done. But you go on out on your rounds and leave it all to me. At least you won't gape like a goldfish tomorrow, now that you know what's coming.' She smiled and gently pushed me out of the kitchen.

I went my rounds that day with my mind half on the morrow, determined to curb my natural awkwardness and to be full of smooth competence. But time and again as I strolled the streets and greeted the parishioners, I found myself blushing in anticipation of some disaster.

The day of the Conference was lowering and wet. The lights were on throughout the presbytery, creating a warm inviting oasis against the gloom outside.

After breakfast, Father Morrison called me into his room. 'Would you mind taking charge of the drinks today, Father?' he asked in his soft Irish accent. 'They all have drinks in here during the actual Conference and then there are the wines with the dinner. Then we'll be back in here afterwards for cards or something. Don't worry. After dinner they'll all just help themselves in here. You just keep an eye open that the bottles and mixers don't run out. Come on, I'll show you where everything is.'

He opened a cupboard underneath his bookcase and began to pull out bottles. Whisky, gin, brandy, sherry, Martini. He placed one of each on a table under his window. 'There are glasses in the next cupboard there, if you'd bring them out.'

Clumsily I did his bidding. As I bent down my glasses slipped off my nose again. I would have to change them or tighten them up. This was getting ridiculous; every time I bent down I would suddenly go blind.

'Not all tumblers,' he said to me. 'You'll need some of those smaller ones for sherry, and the bowl-like ones for brandy. That's fine. Now just arrange them there neatly.'

I would obviously have never made a butler or a wine-waiter.

'Now we need the tonics, gingers, lemonade, water and ice a bit later on.' Again, as if by magic, he produced more bottles from another shelf. I took them from him and arranged them on the table already laden with the spirits and the glasses.

'Would you get a couple of openers from the drawer there? And when you're getting the ice later ask Sadie to cut up a couple of lemons. There now, anything missing?'

I stood in silent amazement, goggling at this vast array. All seemed ready for an alcoholic orgy. I knew Father Morrison kept drink, as he'd offered me one the first night I came.

'Are ye a Pioneer?' he had asked. 'Have you given up the drink?'

'No, no, Father,' I had flustered. 'I just have never seemed to have the chance or the inclination. My mother and father take a drink,' I blundered on. 'But I just never have. Nothing against it.'

I had thought myself moderately seasoned, but this assembly of liquors surpassed anything I had ever seen. There were going to be only twelve of us I knew, and there seemed to be enough drink for a regiment.

'You know where everything is now,' said Father Morrison. 'So if anything looks as though it's running short, you just bring out another bottle. I've got plenty of everything in for them. And take it easy yourself, Dermot,' he added smiling at me. 'You're not used to it like some of these lads and it will go to your head pretty quickly. Come on then, I'll show you where the wines are. You're in charge of them too.'

We moved into the dining room where the table was already laid with immaculate linen and polished silver. Three wine glasses sparkled by each setting.

'Sadie should be working in Buckingham Palace,' I said with some awe.

'Ah, she's a wonderful woman,' said Father Morrison. 'Wait until you taste the food. She surpasses herself completely on Conference day.'

He opened a cupboard in the huge walnut sideboard that dominated one wall of the room. 'The red wines are in here. I've opened several of them so that they can breathe, but there's a corkscrew there if we need any more. The red is with the meat of course, although some of them may just stick to white that we have with the salmon and the soup. They're all in the refrigerator. I'll have them out and opened just before dinner, if you'll serve them out once we get in here.'

I felt a sweat breaking out on me at the thought of my duties, and how many chances they offered for me to make a mess. My fears must have been mirrored in my face, as Father Morrison placed a reassuring hand on my arm.

'Stop worrying for Heaven's sakes. It's only a party. So long as you keep them supplied with plenty of drink they'll not be expecting service up to the standards of the Savoy. It's all very free and easy. Relax and enjoy yourself.'

This repetition of Sadie's encouragement served only to increase my apprehension but I put a brave smile on my face. 'I'll be fine Father,' I said. 'I've just never been to an occasion quite as elaborate as this. Even the Ordination breakfast was all done by somebody else. And I nearly died of nervousness at that.' I managed a snicker which sounded like the lament of an expiring goat.

The rest of the morning I spent in my room. I bobbed down occasionally to the dining room to refresh my memory, or to renew my fears. On one such occasion as I fingered the sets of glasses as though to derive some mystical strength from them, the door from the kitchen burst open and in marched Sadie, a tray full of condiments in her hands. I leapt back from the table as if caught in some shady misdemeanour, snagged my foot in the legs of a chair, and fell flat on my back. My poor glasses as always bounced from my nose.

'Get up out of there Father,' said Sadie, struggling to repress a whoop of laughter. 'Get up and get out of here before you destroy all my work. Settle down for goodness' sake or you'll be a wreck even before they all arrive.'

Shamefacedly, I struggled from the room, but my nerves were still jangled when the cars began to draw up at the door. I went down to Father Morrison's room as though to face a firing squad. But none of the other priests took very much notice of me, and when they did they managed to put me at my ease. I made no mistakes with the drinks, and this and the two sherries I had myself, gave me renewed confidence. During the theological discussion I had sufficient sense not to air any opinion. The practical sense and experience of these men went far beyond any bookish ideas that I could express.

Father Morrison had introduced me to them all as they came in, but as I looked round the circle there were few to whom I could match a name. A Father Fairey I did remember, both because of his odd name and because he was the only other curate. His parish was near Barnsley, a mining town much like our own. He was some years older than me.

In both face and body he strongly resembled an amiable ape, a fact which seemed to cause him no concern.

A little wizened man whose feet dangled a couple of inches from the floor as he perched on his chair, I remembered as Father Clancy. When he smiled, it was as though he was illuminated from within. He smiled often, especially when I offered him another drink. His capacity for whisky was to be a marvel to my inexperience.

But the rest, most of them big burly thickened men, were anonymous to me after the brief introductions. They were all too immersed in the comparisons between their various parishes to have much time for small talk with an unseasoned curate. They were not actively unkind. I suppose they reckoned that there was likely to be little that I could offer, that would be either of interest or advantage to then. Since they were all thirty or forty years older than me, I had to sympathize with their interpretation of the generation gap. It made things very much easier for me.

At dinner I exhibited a deft expertise with the wines which was as much a surprise to me as to anyone else. I was placed near tiny Father Clancy whose capacity for wine was as unlimited as his earlier ability to swig whisky. He was a gay little man with an obviously unbounded enjoyment of life. But as the day wore on, the enormous dinner he had eaten was finding the absorption of the liquor more and more difficult. The excellence of Sadie's food could not match the sheer volume of liquid. My own eyes were moistening and my tongue slightly thickening as I took the opportunity to point out to Father Morrison in a whisper that Father Clancy was getting incapably drunk.

'Don't worry Dermot,' he whispered back. 'He's always like this, poor man. We'll put him to bed in a minute and he'll be as right as rain after a few hours sleep.' As if on signal, one of the burly parish priests at that very moment, picked up Father Clancy as though he were a little doll. 'Come on Paddy,' he soothed as though to a child. 'Have a wee sleep for yourself.'

Another priest opened the door and I heard the great feet moving steadily up the stairs. Nobody made any comment, nor was there the slightest pause in the jokes or the drinking. Only my eyes goggled behind their glasses, only my mouth hung slightly agape.

'Have you got the hang of the game yet?' said the simian Father Fairey to me. 'Come on, try a hand or two. Beginner's luck you know.'

I had, indeed, got the rough pattern of the game, but it was several hands later before I plucked up enough courage to make any bet. Even with four kings I expected to be beaten. But when the final hand was over, and the tea and sandwiches were being tackled, I discovered with some glee that I had actually won five pounds during the evening.

'Don't let it run away with you,' advised Father Fairey. 'I know, because I felt that way too. You'll find if you play at all regularly that you'll somehow lose more than you win. Everybody seems to. Though where the money goes is a bit of a mystery then, isn't it?' He clapped me on the shoulder with such gleeful force, that once again my glasses bounced from my nose. It turned out that he was Father Clancy's curate, so, as all the rest drifted away into the early evening he stayed on until it was time to rouse Father Clancy. There was no awkwardness or surprise when he came down the stairs at about eight o'clock. He had a cup of tea and Father Fairey drove him away.

'Poor Paddy,' said Father Morrison to me as they left. 'I should have told you about him and then it would not have been such a surprise to you. He was driving home one night, totally sober I may say, when an old man stepped right out in front of him. Killed on the spot of course. Paddy blamed himself, though no one else did, and had a complete breakdown. Then he took to the drink. But he's such a lovely fellow, that even the Bishop understands. That's why he sent him Father Fairey to look after him, even though the parish isn't really big enough for two. He never drives himself any more, just refuses to get behind a wheel. A great pity. Poor Paddy.'

There was nothing to say except to thank Father Morrison for telling me. Paddy Clancy had seemed to me such a happy little man with not a worry in the world. Maybe that would teach me not to judge people on first impressions. Maybe that would teach me too to be careful about getting a taste for the drink. I fell about the place quite enough without falling about with drink.

The very next morning as I was preparing to go out, there was a ring on the bell. Sadie came to tell me that there was a man wanting to see me. He was in the waiting room. 'He smells awfully of drink Father,' she said with some alarm. 'At this time in the morning too.'

'Probably somebody wanting money for more drink,' I replied. I had already met several of these, who regard the presbytery or the priest as an endless source of drink money.

The man in the waiting room was shrunken, grey and shabby. The smell of what even I recognised as methylated spirits was overpowering. But it was not money he wanted.

'I'm drunk again Father,' he said, 'and I'm ashamed of it. I want you to give me the Pledge Father, so that I'll never touch the filthy stuff again.'

'The Pledge,' I repeated. 'But I don't have any Pledge forms, or the words or anything.'

'That's no problem Father,' he said. 'Just give me the Pledge. Please Father.' He was almost weeping.

'All right then,' I said, distinctly taken aback by his passionate urge for virtue. 'Just kneel down there and repeat after me.'

I hastily invented a form of words in my mind. 'I do solemnly promise . . .'

'I do solemnly promise . . .'

'To Almighty God . . .'

'To Almighty God . . .'

'That from this time onwards . . .'

'That from this time onwards . . .'

It suddenly struck me that I was issuing this promise to the Almighty as well, and that though I would heed the warnings of Father Morrison and the example of poor Father Clancy, I had no wish to give up drink altogether. So I made a hasty mental reservation and informed the Lord that these words did not apply to me.

'I will not touch alcoholic drink . . .'

'I will not touch alco . . . alcoholic drink . . .'

'And I ask for Your help . . .'

'And I ask for Your help . . .'

'God bless you Father. That's great. I've taken the Pledge now. Isn't that great?' He stumbled out the door cackling and, I've no doubt, went straight to the nearest pub.

# CHAPTER SIX

ONE of the sadder spots in our parish was a Home, run by nuns, for unmarried mothers. The girls were admitted when they were six months pregnant, either because they had no one to look after them, or because their families wanted them out of the way to avoid any scandal. Where they could, they paid towards their keep, and whether they paid or not, they were expected to take a full share of all the household work. The assumption was that their babies would be offered for adoption immediately after birth.

The Home itself was a beautiful old house set in spacious grounds. It had been redesigned to meet the more functional need it now supplied, was spotlessly clean and polished, and comfortably furnished. A chapel had been incorporated into the building, and indeed it was there that I had said my first Midnight Mass at Christmas. It was an odd place to celebrate the birthday of the most famous baby of all, as the birth of all other babies there brought more sorrow to their mothers than joy.

The girls were nearly all young, sixteen to eighteen; the turnover was rapid, as four to five months was the maximum stay. About them all was the same air of resigned misery. The nuns treated them well and medically they had good care, but there was always the underlying air of guilt and punishment. When my natural diffidence was added to their sadness, conversation became very difficult. I went there regularly, because so few other visitors ever called, but I did not look forward to my visits, nor, I am sure, did I spread much joy or light. Motherhood and birth there were such a contrast to their looked-for, welcomed, and joyous counterparts in marriage.

Not all unmarried mothers went there of course. Some rejoiced in their maternity, married or not, and lovingly looked forward to the birth of their children whom they would bring up with just as much affection as any married mother. Others rather more stoically just accepted their fate and ignored the hostility or insults of their neighbours. They too would keep their children, although the bitterness engendered in them by the ostracism to which they were often subjected, boded ill for the future happiness of their children.

Mary Smith fitted into none of these categories. Mary was a big raw-boned freckle cheeked girl of remarkable ugliness. Her ginger hair sprouted in ridiculous disarray. When I first called at her parents' home, she blurted out the fact of her pregnancy with no apparent embarrassment or shame. My first reaction, which I quickly stifled, was to laugh out loud. I wondered uncharitably how anyone could have found poor Mary sufficiently attractive to create the possibility of fathering a child on her.

'What I want to know Father,' she said aggressively, 'is what help t'Church gives to girls like me? I've 'eard that there are funds specially for us. Can I apply, and how do I go about it?'

I was taken aback. I had never heard of any such funds, nor had I ever heard of anyone seeking to make some money out of this particular misfortune. 'Well, I don't really know Mary,' I replied. 'I know we have homes where you can go for a few months, and have the baby adopted.'

'Oh no,' she burst in. 'I'm not going to one of those bloody places, wi't' nuns looking down their noses at you all the time. And I'm going to keep the little brat. It'll be me that's gone through it all, and I'm not going to let one of them toffee-nosed women who're too stupid or scared to have one of their own, get all the rewards of my pains.' An odd attitude, I thought, and of dubious logic, but rather admirable for all that. A tough and uncompromising lady, our Mary.

'But if it's money you want Mary to have, and help you keep the child, what about the father? If need be, you can take him to court and get some maintenance. But doesn't he want to help, or might he not even marry you? May I ask who he is?'

For the first time Mary's eyes were cast down and a faint flush spread over her cheeks. 'Well it's like this Father,' she said. 'It were dark and I don't know who he was. He were in the army,' she added almost defiantly. 'He were a sergeant, I could feel the stripes.'

Had I not been sitting down, I swear I would have fallen. I gulped, grunted and fell silent. After a long pause, I risked my voice. 'Look Mary, just leave it with me. I'll talk with Father Morrison, with your permission, and see what can be done. Have you got a job now?'

'Yes, I work in a shop in Barnsley,' she said. 'But they'll get rid of me as soon as t'baby becomes noticeable. Everyone knows I'm not married you see, and they wouldn't think it proper.'

Poor Mary, her one brief encounter with an unknown striped soldier, had turned her world inside out. Her parents seemed unperturbed by the situation. There was no reproach or unkindness, but they were obviously prepared to allow Mary to paddle her own canoe.

I mentioned the matter to Father Morrison that evening at supper. He too seemed surprised that it was Mary who was a victim. Her slip from moral values might be par for the course, but that anyone could have glimpsed romance in Mary's unprepossessing person was harder to fathom.

'There certainly are no special funds for unmarried pregnant girls,' he said. 'You were quite right there. And I can understand her not wanting to go to the Home, however good the Sisters are. I suppose there's no chance of tracing the anonymous sergeant?' he mused. 'It reminds me of a case I once had in Malaya when I was an army chaplain. Did you know I'd been an army chaplain? That's where I first picked up this weird bug that does all sorts of queer things to me.

'Anyway. This girl from a local Malayan village came along to the colonel of our lot, claiming that one of our lads was the father of the child she had just had. She even named him, a wild Scots chap I remember. I even remember his name, McCluskey. Since he was a Catholic, the colonel asked me if I'd deal with the matter, arrange maintenance of the child if it was his, and so on. I called in McCluskey. He made no attempt to deny that he'd been with the girl, but claimed that so had half the battalion. There was no reason he said why the child should be his rather than any of the others! I went along with him anyway to see the girl. Now McCluskey had a head of violent ginger hair and there before us on the head of this poor little brown, slant-eyed Malayan baby was a thatch of exactly the same orange hair. It looked most odd. I turned to McCluskey and shrugged. Paternity was obvious. "Could it be a coincidence Father?" he said. A coincidence, ha!' He burst into that wild laughter that I'd last heard when Jasper led me into his room, that first night. When the fit had subsided, he turned back to the subject of Mary.

'All this is no great help to her,' he said. 'Just leave it with me for a while and I'll think of something.'

'Thank you very much Father,' I said. 'Sorry I can't deal with things myself without worrying you.'

He smiled off any worry.

It was about a week later when he brought up the subject again. 'I've been thinking about poor Mary. There's only one thing we can do. When she loses the job in Barnsley, we'll bring her in here. Sadie could do with some help. This place is far too big just for her even with the cleaning lady coming in twice a week. So we'll employ her here. She's a fine strong lassie and some hard work will do her no harm at all even in the last few months. Then when she's had the baby she can either stay on if she wants, or get another job that pays more money.'

'That's wonderfully good of you Father. I'm sure she'll be delighted. But won't it cause a lot of gossip, especially if she's staying here?'

'Och gossip be damned,' he said. This was the first and only time I ever heard him swear. 'And she won't be staying here. There isn't room. And Sadie values her evening privacy too much. Gossip,' he snorted. 'Wasn't there gossip when Jesus helped Mary Magdalene? And did He care?'

And so it was settled. When Mary's protuberance grew very pronounced she was duly dismissed from her job in Barnsley and came along to us. She was willing if very clumsy, and she got clumsier and clumsier as she grew in size. She was huge and seemed to grow more ginger and disarrayed by the day. But she was grateful – frighteningly grateful. She caught me one day as I was coming in for lunch.

'It's going to be a boy you know Father,' she said. 'I'm sure of it. And I want to show how thankful I am to you and Father Morrison by calling him after you. So what are your names Father?'

I winced. What would the gossip be then, if not only did we take in an unmarried girl, but then had the baby named after us? But mindful of Father Morrison's charity I put a warm smile on my face.

'That's very nice of you, Mary,' I said. 'Well, Father Morrison's name is John and mine is Dermot, which really isn't a common name in this part you know.'

'All the better,' she crowed in triumph. 'That's it then. Dermot John Smith. That's a lovely name isn't it? Oh, it will have to be a boy now.'

My name first, I reflected gloomily. All the talk is going to be about me. John could be anyone, but there was only one Dermot as far as I knew, in miles. I groaned, even though I tried to take this new burden of the Lord with resigned acceptance. Father Morrison, of course, found it hilarious and issued his manic roar of joy yet again.

Doctor Murphy had undertaken to care for her, and he arranged the hospital bed and had a whip-round for baby clothes for her, while Maeve, his wife, childless as she was herself, filled poor Mary with all the best advice. They too were hysterical about the choice of name. Maeve took the opportunity to lean on my shoulder, pat me on the back, stroke my arm. It was all getting too much for me.

When Mary went into hospital, she was a mere four hours in labour, and with the minimum of difficulty produced a healthy bouncing boy. It had to be a boy of course.

'It's rather peculiar,' said Doctor Murphy to us. 'Wait until you see him.'

'What do you mean, peculiar?' I said with apprehension. I had a horrible feeling that by some weird accident it might look like me.

'Just wait and see,' chuckled the doctor. 'It'll surprise you, I'll bet.'

Father Morrison had offered us both a drink to wet the baby's head. I swallowed mine in a gulp and rushed out as though I were indeed the father straining to see his new born child. I lamely explained that since both her parents were working, and the unknown father was unlikely to appear, I'd better pay a visit lest she feel deserted. Their chuckles followed me from the room.

The bike ride to the hospital was accomplished in much less than my normal time. I rushed to the maternity ward where my fraught appearance alarmed the Sister into saying, 'There's no emergency Father. You must have the wrong ward.'

'No, no Sister,' I said with a ghastly attempt at a smile. 'There's nothing wrong, no rush, no emergency.' I was almost gasping with fright as I pushed past her. 'I just came to congratulate Mary Smith. Mary, you know. She works for us.'

'She's at the end of the ward there Father,' said the Sister looking at me most strangely.

'Thank you, thank you Sister.'

I was almost sobbing as I loped frenziedly down the ward, seeing none of the other mothers, responding to none of their 'Hallo Fathers.' I didn't even look at Mary beaming with ginger pride. My eyes glued themselves to the little bundle she held so fondly in the crook of her arm. Dermot John Smith was as brown as a berry and had lovely almond shaped eyes. Though they fixed unseeingly on me and gurgles of apparent content bubbled from his wee brown mouth, I felt obliged to sit down on the chair by the bed in a mixture of relief and astonishment.

'He's Chinese Mary,' I said, unable to raise my eyes from the little mite. 'The Chinese army hasn't been here has it? There aren't any Chinese in the British Army are there? There aren't any Chinese sergeants here? It must be a mistake.'

At last I looked at Mary. She was beaming, her poor homely face transformed with motherly love.

'No mistake Father,' she laughed. 'I was there when it was born remember. It's as much a surprise to me as to you. But it's mine alright. Dermot John Smith.'

'Ha!' I jumped about a foot from the chair, and said very belatedly, 'Congratulations Mary. A lovely child.'

I pumped her hand and moved dazedly back down the ward, again impervious to the women and their greetings, oblivious even of the Sister. I rode my bike home in a state of numbness.

Doctor Murphy was still drinking Father Morrison's whisky as I walked in. 'You need another one,' said Father Morrison as he and the doctor roared with delight at my appearance. 'Here, drink that, and stop looking so appalled.'

I shook myself like a dog and gulped down the whisky again.

'We've worked it all out,' said Father Morrison. 'Do you remember about nine months ago when they had that Army Exhibition in Barnsley. A recruitment drive really. Well one of the groups brought here to rouse interest was a troop of Gurkhas. One of them must have chanced across Mary and there's the wee soul named after you. Dermot John Smith is a Gurkha.'

I don't know which of the three of us came out of our paroxysm of laughter first. I do know I needed another whisky. Gurkha Dermot John Smith.

## CHAPTER SEVEN

WHEN Mary came out of hospital, she took just a few days rest at home before returning to her duties with us. In a mixture of pride and gratitude she had decided to eschew the chance of more lucrative employment, and give her all to her new-found family. Her decision was accepted with resignation by Father Morrison and myself, with some annoyance by Sadie.

'I have to work harder because she's here,' she complained to me. 'It takes such a time to explain to her what to do, and then keep checking to see whether she's doing it properly, that I'd save time and energy just doing it myself in the first place. It's all right you two being full of Christian charity, but I'm the one who has to carry the can.'

I had to acknowledge the justice of her remarks. We all suffered from Mary's misguided zeal. I could never find socks, handkerchiefs or underwear. They would be there somewhere, but it was hunt the thimble until they were found. And twice I had nearly broken a leg on a stretch of polished wood on the landing which Mary had lavishly covered with wax polish. Procedure exactly right, except that she had omitted to rub the polish in, and the surface in consequence had all the qualities of somewhat tacky ice. She was so anxious, so hurt when anything went wrong.

'Look Sadie,' I said, overcome by a flash of inspiration. 'Why don't you take advantage of Mary's return and go and have a little holiday for yourself. It's months since you even had a proper day off. There must be somewhere you can go and if you haven't enough money I can lend you some.'

'You're very kind Father,' replied Sadie. 'But I won't need your money. Thank you anyway. But the break sounds like a good idea.' She leant back in her chair her eyes far away. Her face softened somehow, and I could see the years roll away, see Sadie as she must have been when she was a young girl. I did not dare to disturb the moment.

'There is a place I've been meaning to go back to for years.' She spoke slowly almost reverently. 'It's near Clevedon in Somerset, just a village with a little pub, a shop, a few houses. I used to go there when I was younger.'

There was almost a fierceness in her voice as she straightened up and said, 'You're quite right Father. I need a break and that's the very place. What day is it? Wednesday. Right I'll see Father Morrison and I'll go on Monday after the weekend. If I'm back on the Saturday, well Mary can't kill you in a week can she?'

I wasn't at all sure about that. The threat to us from Mary's presence seemed untied to any natural calender. But I smiled happily at Sadie. At long last I had done something that seemed worthwhile.

'That's great Sadie. And don't be hurrying back after a week. I'm sure Father won't mind how long you stay, and we'll survive Mary somehow.'

'No, a week's quite enough Father. I'll be back on the Saturday.'

And so Sadie went away on the Monday and we were left to the tender mercies of Mary. She didn't kill us, but she had several excellent attempts. She burned our boiled eggs. Burned them! She set a frying-pan on fire and had not Father Morrison happened to go into the kitchen would probably have burned herself, the kitchen and even the house to a crisp. After that we went out for lunch and supper every day. Breakfast we just lived through. Every day she brought her Eastern baby to the house, which Sadie would never allow, and we were treated to the normal cacophany and chaos with which all babies seem to surround themselves. A further trial to my timid soul was Mary's habit ever and anon, of freeing one large globular breast from its constraints and stuffing it into little Dermot's ever receptive mouth. Unalloyed delight wreathed his little brown face, as I turned purple and fled. I began to think that she did it deliberately to embarrass me.

It was therefore with profound relief that I greeted Sadie when she returned on the Saturday evening. Amos had been to collect her from the station in his old banger, and he shared the delight with which she was welcomed. Even Mary, her baby safely left behind this time, received her as though her return marked the end of a spell in the Siberian salt mines. The normal tranquillity of our life was restored and poor Mary's disasters faded into fond memory.

Some days passed before I chanced to be alone with Sadie. She insisted that I sit in the comfortable armchair in her kitchen and that I accept a cup of tea. Suitably ensconced I said to her, 'How did the holiday go Sadie? Did it bring back all the good old memories?'

She sat gazing into space in much the same posture as she had assumed that night I first suggested the holiday. Again I felt constrained to sit silent and still.

'I can never be grateful enough to you Father,' she said eventually.

'But all I did was suggest you go away for a while Sadie.' I was rather nonplussed by this effusive response to what had been after all nothing more than one of my very rare bright ideas.

'Father,' she said, 'you have helped me to lay a ghost. A ghost that has been haunting me these thirty years. I would never have plucked up courage to do it myself, but you made me do it. I could kiss you.'

'Ha!' I jumped up in alarm.

'Sit down Father,' she soothed, 'I won't, I promise you. Just sit down and let me tell you about it. I've never spoken to anybody all these years, and I've just got to tell someone now because I feel so much better, so alive for the first time in all those years.'

Sadie indeed looked a different person. I had always seen her as a thin little soul in every way, kind and efficient, but with no passion burning through her veins. Life, real life, even as lived in Brimley, seemed to have passed Sadie by. Yet here she was sitting in front of me vibrant, glowing. Something dramatic had happened in that unlikely little village in Somerset. As her tale unfolded, yet again did I rue my habit of looking solely at the surface of people. I surely should have enough experience by this time to know that a world of life teems below even the most placid surface. One of the more ridiculous aspects of this blinkered view of mine had been that I had never tried to put an age on Sadie. It came as somewhat of a shock to me to realize that she was not yet fifty. Sadie had been born and brought up in Bristol. Again it had never occurred to me to try to identify the obviously non-Yorkshire burr in her voice. In the throes of the Depression she had been fortunate enough, or efficient enough I suspect, to get a job as a secretary in a printing firm. One of the young printers employed in the same firm was Frank. Frank McEvoy, a Catholic like herself, was the last boy of a big family originally from Ireland.

'He was the image of you Father,' she added to my consternation. 'A big awkward-looking lad with a heart of gold. Shy, he was so shy, he'd blush if anyone looked at him.'

Sadie was certain from the first moment she saw him, that he was the man for her. It seems to have taken some considerable persuasion to break through his reserve, and to get him actually to take her out. But within a very short time, it appeared, Frank was as head over heels in love with Sadie, as she was with him. They exchanged visits to each other's families, and though courtship was expected to be more leisurely than in our frenzied age, they became engaged within the year. The year was 1939. They were both twenty two years old.

With an enterprise that was probably remarkable in those days, they decided to find a place to live at some remove from their families, yet near enough to keep contact and to be able to travel to their work. They found the ideal spot in the little village of Clockton between Bristol and Clevedon. On the sea, yet peacefully rustic, it seemed an ideal place to start their life together. An old cottage was for sale, their little savings enough to put down a deposit. Renovations were needed but Frank was clever with his hands.

During the long lovely summer of 1939 they went down to their house every weekend, Saturday and Sunday, bringing the place into the kind of order and shape that they wanted. For the restoration of the thatch roof they recruited the help of a local farm worker, who seemed, from Sadie's naïve description, to have been more than somewhat in love with her himself. The old beams and the rough plaster of the walls they restored themselves, bringing that lovely chintzy air to the cottage which nowadays is so much a selling point. Inevitably they made friends with nearly all the villagers so that they would eventually move into an already secure and friendly atmosphere. Life was good, their hopes and future certain.

The dark clouds of war which gathered inexorably during that glorious summer seem to have been ignored by them as by so many others. There was a general almost fatalistic presumption that just as war had loomed and disappeared in 1938, so it would again in 1939. The patent anguish of Neville Chamberlain on September the third was numbly reflected in the majority of people. Sadie and Frank went ahead and fixed their wedding date for just before Christmas. Even when Frank was called-up in late September and sent to France in November, they still presumed that nothing would interfere with their happiness. Sadie continued to go down to the cottage to add those warm personal touches which would complete their joy. And when Frank was guaranteed a week's leave for the wedding by his commanding officer, life was as full and satisfying as it could be.

'I just can't remember the exact details of what happened Father,' she said slowly. Her face and her voice had clouded and the beaming youthful joy of the earlier recital had disappeared. 'I do know there was a telegram to Frank's parents a couple of days before he was due to come on leave for the wedding. I never saw the telegram, so I don't know what the words were. Frank's father came down to our house, and as soon as I saw him, I knew. That part of the war was later to be known as the "phoney war" Father. There was no real fighting in France at all. But every now and again each side fired a few shells just to remind the others that they were there. Frank was on guard duty near an ammunition dump when one of those odd shells came whistling over. It landed right on the dump. They never found even a hair of his head, poor lad. Not even anything to bury. Poor, poor Frank.'

There was a long pause while Sadie tried to recover her

composure. When she did start again it was in matter of fact tones as though the agony and loss were mastered.

'I never did go back to the cottage. I got it sold, and as soon as I could I moved away from Bristol, as though the pain would go because I'd put space between myself and where I'd been so happy. I came up here, worked in a factory, worked in an office, after the war. But there was never any sense of belonging, no happiness, no life really. I just existed. I knew Father Morrison as a curate when he came back from the war, and when he became parish priest here, he asked me if I'd come with him as housekeeper. He knew all about the war and the suffering. I think he knows about Frank, though he's never mentioned it. And how he found out I'll never know, because I've never spoken to a soul about it since I left Bristol.'

Her pause this time was gentle and full of the warm gratitude she obviously felt towards the kindly priest who had given life back to her. Not the life she would obviously have had with Frank, but at least a reason to live after the long empty years.

'And then you came Father. I nearly died that first night when you walked through the door. I was so glad that Jasper made a nuisance of himself. It just gave me time to pull myself together before I was introduced to you. I've no idea what I said. I was in a daze. It was almost as though Frank had come back to me after all those years. There are all sorts of differences when I look at you closely. He had black hair and brown eyes and I don't think he was quite as tall as you. But that first impression was frightening. And it's since you came that for the first time really I've let myself think about Frank. And you know Father, it has brought not sorrow but peace and acceptance. I'd even let myself think about Clockton and the cottage. And when you suggested I go on a holiday, I knew at once where I had to go.'

She had stayed in the little village pub, walked past the cottage, though she never went in. She visited Frank's brothers and sisters and her own, and was back now with all ghosts laid.

'I've been so silly all these years Father, and I'm so grateful to you for making me go. I even went to the church where we were going to be married, and I lit a candle for Frank, God rest him, and for you.'

I squirmed uneasily in my chair, coughed a couple of unnecessary times to cover the fact that my eyes were misting over. I could think of absolutely nothing to say.

'Get on with you now Father, encouraging an old woman in her bletherings. You're only keeping me from my work, and I'm sure you've got better things to do as well.'

'Yes, well,' I finally grunted. 'Good night then Sadie, and . . . er . . . thank you very much. I feel very honoured.'

'Away with you,' she said and bundled me out of the kitchen. I smiled absurdly to myself as I went up to my own room. Just a reaction to the warmth and character of a lovely and loving lady. We never mentioned the matter again, either of us. But even Father Morrison noticed the change. 'I've never seen Sadie so happy,' he said one night at dinner. 'I think she must be in love!'

Oh yes Sadie was in love as she had always been. A calm gentle and rewarding love, at last.

# CHAPTER EIGHT

If in other areas of life I was slowly acquiring some confidence, in mixing with the self-styled 'upper crust' I was still as gauche and uncomfortable as I had ever been. It was their composure that I envied, and which produced in me not only a sense of inferiority, but on occasion, considerable irritation. Not that Brimley's 'upper crust' was large in numbers. Mining villages did not as a rule have a large scale aristocracy. They were not that kind of small town. But on the hills above the town facing away towards open country, rather than on to the bleakness of the industrial area, there were a number of largish mansions. Their owners were not of course all Catholics, but they clung together as in a club, and to meet one or two was to run the risk of being regarded as a member of the club by all the others.

Since doctors seemed to be automatic choices for membership it was through the Murphys that I became involved. Neither Tom nor Maeve, give them their due, were the natural snobs that formed most of the membership. They were elected for their status rather than their character. Indeed Tom bitterly lampooned his fellows-elect, and even to their faces. They loved him for it. 'You'll just have to meet Tom Murphy, Dr Tom Murphy. He's a great wit. You'll love him.'

Maeve moved among them like a large-breasted Mother Earth, sensually cajoling and guiding them. But they never knew how to take me. I sat on their hats, or dropped their cups, or put whisky in my wine, as if inspired by some manic force. I brayed with laughter at the wrong times, forgot the point of any story I might be bold enough to begin. They tolerated me only because of the Murphys. Tom would have punished them cruelly had there been any snide criticism.

I had been worried about going to their houses, but Father Morrison had eased my fears, and indeed suggested to me that I should regard it as my duty to bring some breath of Christian air among them.

'But I'm sure I'll only make them laugh at the Church Father,' I protested. 'You know me. I'm hardly likely to rouse any love or respect for the Church in them.'

'Don't you worry about that,' said Father Morrison. 'You just throw your bread upon the waters and leave the rest to the Lord.' Reluctantly, and as rarely as was consonant with good manners, I continued my mission to these lords of the earth. My visits, however infrequent, came to the unlikely ears of Matt McGinley.

'Ha,' he roared at me on one of my equally infrequent visits to him, on my way to Nellie Ryan. 'I see you're up to the usual Church games. Hobnobbing with the rich, and to hell with all the poor people. I should never have been fooled by your innocent appearance. You're just the same as the rest of them. And when the revolution comes you'll disappear like chaff before the reaper, along of all them rich ones.' His garbled use of the Scripture always managed to disconcert me. I opened my mouth to explain and defend myself. 'Off with you. Get out of this house,' he bellowed. 'You're in here under false pretences. You're a sheep in lamb's clothing or whatever it is. Out.'

My embarrassment was a mixture of shame at being cast out of the house, and apprehension that there might indeed be some truth in what he was saying. The whole situation was thoroughly unpleasant. But that didn't make it go away.

Ever since that first visit of mine to his house Tom had been very precise about visiting Father Morrison every week. He was obviously of the opinion that the Father's health gave grounds for far more concern than Father Morrison himself would ever admit. I did my best to ease his burdens but he would never discuss his health with me, as I presume he had with my predecessor Father Mullin – not surprisingly, as Father Mullin, whom I met occasionally when he too came to visit Father Morrison, was a mature man who now had his own parish. It was obvious that Father Morrison found him very much easier company than he did the gawky tongue-tied stranger that was me.

On this particular Wednesday morning, after his check-up on Father Morrison, Tom came up to my room. The rain was lashing from the skies and I had decided to leave my visiting until such time as it eased. Nobody that I knew of was in such dire straits as to demand that I soak myself to the skin to lighten their load. Truth to tell I was dozing in my armchair when the knock came on the door, and I shot to my feet with a look of wild alarm as Tom came in.

'God help us Father,' he said. 'You look as though I'm the Devil himself hotfoot from hell. Sit down man or you'll have a seizure.'

'Sorry Doctor . . . er . . . Tom. I must have dozed off in the chair, and I didn't know where I was when you knocked. Is something wrong? Father Morrison? He's bad is he?' I was stammering with anticipation.

'Will you calm down Father,' said Tom. 'Can't a man come to see you without it being disaster? Father Morrison is no worse or better than he always is. I just like to keep an eye on him as you never know when he might take a bad turn. No, I've come to see you, with an invitation.'

'An invitation?' I repeated. 'What do you mean, an invitation?'

'There you go again Father. An invitation is an invitation. Not a summons from the K.G.B., or the Black Spot. You're an awful man for worrying. It'll be your heart and blood pressure I'll be attending to next.'

I blushed at his laughing rebuke. Why did I always go off the handle even before I knew what was happening? Yet again I made the resolve to be suave and polished, to imitate the composure of his friends up the hill. But his very next words set off yet another attack of the dithers.

'Charlie and Freda Broadbent are having a bit of a "do" tomorrow night and they'd like you to come.'

'Ha,' I shrieked. Charlie and Freda Broadbent were the ones of all the group of whom I stood most in awe. Charlie was the owner and managing director of a firm, of toolmakers I think, which he had inherited from his father. He had been to the best schools, spoke with a 'refeened' accent, and lived in the biggest and most ornate of the mansions. Freda had obviously been chosen as a mate because of her background and connections rather than for any physical attraction. 'County' oozed from every one of her large and obvious pores. She spoke and looked like a thoroughbred horse. I had been in their house once before with Tom when he had been called to see their gardener's wife who happened to be a Catholic. Indeed, it was in that house that I had carefully perched my awkward body on top of a hat belonging to Mrs Broadbent, a floral creation which I had rapidly reduced to something that resembled a herbaceous border after a roller had passed over it. And now to go to a 'do'! I'd die with embarrassment.

'A "do",' I said in a strangled yelp. 'At Charlie and Freda Broadbent's?'

'Yes Father,' said Tom with some impatience. 'At Charlie and Freda Broadbent's. Tomorrow night. There'll be a buffet, some drinks. You'll meet some people. You need people, you know, Father. You can't spend your life grunting in monosyllables with the likes of Amos amd Matt McGinley. So pull yourself together, get on your best bib and tucker. Maeve and I will pick you up at half-seven. Maeve will be driving. It's my night off and I'm going to get quite royally plastered. And we'll look after you and bring you back home. All you've got to do is to look half as intelligent as you are, and occasionally behave as though you've heard the English language before. It'll do you the world of good. Take you out of yourself.'

'Ha!' I repeated.

'Oh for God's sake stop that roaring Father. I'm not asking you to kiss a leper. Just to have a few drinks, some nice food, and meet some pleasant people. There are times when I despair of you. Tell you what. Come up to our place on your own about half-six. I'll get a few belts inside you before you go and you won't feel a thing.'

I had no defence. I agreed, though with fear gnawing at my vitals. I tried to persuade myself that it was scruples at leading a life unsuited to a priest, but I knew that it was simple terror. Tom Murphy went out sighing at my crassness.

'You be at our place at half-six, mind,' was his parting warning.

I did not have a best bib and tucker in any ordinary sense. But at least I put on my other suit that did not have quite as many gravy stains on the lapels. I polished my shoes and by six o'clock I was in a state of nerves bordering on dementia. Both Sadie and Father Morrison tried to reassure me, but the sweat was gleaming on my forehead still, as I left the house to walk to the Murphys'.

Maeve billowed in an elegant floating creation which emphasized her soft ripeness. Tom also, whose normal appearance was somewhat dishevelled, stood radiant in a beautifully cut lounge suit. I say 'stood' but 'swayed' would be better. Whether to drown his own nervousness, which I could hardly believe, or simply to begin his enjoyment of the evening as early as possible, he gave every appearance of jolly inebriation. 'Great stuff Father,' he slurred happily. 'Come and have a drink.' He poured a whisky for me in which the Queen Mary could have floated, and presented it to me with a royal air.

'Drink that,' he said. 'That'll cure all your nerves. Nothing to be nervous about anyway. Nice people. Good party. Enjoy yourself. Eh Maeve?' He sat down rather abruptly as he turned towards his wife. Apparently any slight change of direction was rather more than his legs could cope with.

Maeve smiled indulgently and patted me affectionately on the arm. I flinched instinctively and poured almost half the whisky down my trouser leg.

'I'm most terribly sorry. My fault. No harm done.' I was beginning to sound more drunk than Tom, and as if to give reality to that appearance, I shot the rest of the whisky down my throat. All that happened was that I became purple in the face, as well as dripping from my left leg.

'Cheers,' I managed to croak.

'Have another,' said Tom bounding to his feet and sloshing another vast measure into my glass.

'Cheers again,' I said weakly and threw it too down my suffering throttle. For a brief moment I thought I would die, and then I too, as if hit across the calves with a stout stick, collapsed into a chair.

'You two make a lovely pair to take a lady to a party,' gurgled Maeve. 'Come on now both of you before I have to call for stretchers for you.' We both rose somewhat unsteadily and seemed to duplicate on our faces a grimace of idiot pleasure. Maeve linked one on either side of her and towed us out to the car.

'Going to be a lovely party,' said Tom, desperately trying to focus his eyes. 'I'll take care of you Father, don't you worry.'

'No problem Tom. Going to be a lovely party. Feel better if I could control the old feet.' I grinned inanely. 'Don't think I'll be dancing.' This struck me as the funniest statement since Groucho Marx, and I brayed with laughter.

'You just stay by me Father,' said Maeve, a smile of beatific joy wreathing her face. 'I'll make sure you meet the right people. You need someone to look after you and Tom can always look after himself.' The big Humber purred away into the comforting darkness. Tom had begun to snore gently and I fixed my eyes on Maeve as though I were a glazed pig's head. The journey took less than five minutes, not nearly enough to restore sanity to my addled wits. I had sufficient sense left to know that the whiskies had nearly paralysed me, sufficient strength to resolve to be even more proper than the occasion demanded. I bounded from the car as though to relieve Mafeking, shook myself like a wet collie and stood as near to attention as was possible.

After some seconds I became aware that I was still alone outside the car. With a clarity I did not know that I possessed, I concluded that something was amiss. I turned very deliberately back to the car. Maeve was just giving Tom a resounding crack on the cheek as I opened the door. His eyelids shot up, he jerked like a puppet and snuffled vaguely. 'Ha,' he said, 'we're here then. Good. What are we all waiting for. Forward the buffs. Charge!' he roared.

We made an entrance that would have aroused interest

during the San Francisco earthquake. Maeve, majestic as always, had a shuffling, mumbling Tom on her right arm, and on the left, marching as stiff as a grenadier, myself. Freda and Charlie Broadbent who came to meet us, showed not the slightest surprise or dismay. Freda took immediate charge of the mumbling Tom, shoved a glass in his hand, and led him to a sumptuous settee. She had scarcely manoeuvred him into a sitting position before the gentle snores began again and he was asleep. She swept the glass from his hand with the same expedition with which she had placed it there seconds earlier, moved back across to Maeve and myself and pushed it into my hand.

'Whisky do you, Father?' she said brightly. 'I know yours is gin, Maeve. I'll bring you one directly.' A ravishing beam lit her horsey face and she was away. This was the test, I thought. Mustn't make a fool of myself. Calm dignity. I raised the glass with exquisite care and slugged the large measure straight back. Lowered the potent arm, shuddered gently, resumed my posture as though I were a Palace Guard at Versailles. I tried to comment to Maeve on how well I was behaving myself, but managed only, 'Haash.'

'Come on Father,' said Maeve maternally. 'I'll introduce you to some people.'

I moved in a haze through a throng of people all laughing merrily and enjoying themselves hugely. I was a model of decorum until I realized that at each encounter I was profering to my new found friends, not a warmly welcoming hand, but an empty glass.

'So shorry, so shorry,' I said dropping it neatly on the floor.

'Have another,' said Freda, who appeared on that instant. She presented Maeve with her gin, and stuck another full glass of whisky in my already outstretched fingers. 'Enjoying yourself are you?' as she disappeared.

'Jolly nice of you to come Father,' said Charlie. 'Nice to see the Church taking an interest in us ordinary people. Ha, ha, ha,' he brayed as he too disappeared. Everybody seemed to be disappearing. The room was revolving slowly so that in no time at all we were back with Tom. He had woken up, was clutching a new glass, and conversing somewhat unsteadily with a little old man. Just as we arrived this little man uttered a deep sigh and collapsed on to the sofa, where he began to snore. It must be the sleeping sofa I decided, and nodded my head so firmly in agreement with my own thought, that once again I poured a steady stream of whisky over my trousers, the right leg this time. 'My trousers will be drunker than I am,' I tried to say, but all I could hear was, 'Hargh, aargh, aargh.' I sat down next to Tom to try to reassure him.

'Newted,' he kept saying. 'All newted. Disgrashful. Terrible people.' I patted him to indicate my agreement and knocked his glass out of his hand.

'Aargh,' I said with some feeling. We sat there murmuring these moving statements to each other. We seemed to be there for hours watching the room and the people and the glasses revolve and revolve. Maeve, who had let me slide on to the sofa and then gone off to join the revolving crowd, now returned, eyes wide with delight.

'Come on my bonny Boy Scouts, time to go to beddy-byes. Just a little drunky are we. Good good. It's very relaxing. Takes away all the inhibitions doesn't it, Father?'

'Newted,' replied Tom.

'Aargh,' was my agreement.

She guided us to the door where Freda and Charlie materialized yet again.

'Thanks very much,' said Maeve. 'Lovely party, wasn't it darling?'

'Aargh,' said Tom.

'Aargh,' I agreed warmly.

The journey to the car was swift and efficient. Tom had decided to join my army, and he too marched in full array. Unfortunately, as I bent to open the car door, my glasses fell from my nose. Both Tom and I began a search with military precision on our knees. We recovered the glasses but neither of us could rise. Since we were below the level of the windows Maeve thought we had disappeared. The weird croaks, which were all that we could issue from our throats, did not penetrate to her as she sat behind the wheel. The car door slammed as she emerged. She rounded the bonnet and tripped immediately over the prostrate Tom who by this time had decided to go to sleep again. Lunging forward she landed the whole of her soft billowing weight on my defenceless person as I struggled to rise.

'Aargh,' grunted Tom as he woke under the pressure of the trip.

'Aargh,' with deep and painful feeling I said, with the last breath in my body.

A warm throaty chuckle emerged from Maeve as she lay unharmed across the pair of us. 'What on earth are you both doing down here? Come on you silly boys, get up out of that and let's go home.' She pushed herself up, grinding my head more firmly into the gravel. First to Tom and then to me she extended the rounded curve of her arm, and somehow we both arose. With a manoeuvre as unplanned as it was delicate, Tom bundled himself into the back seat, while I collapsed into the front, surrounded by the heady perfume of Maeve.

'I'll drop you off first Tom,' she said, 'so stay awake. And then I'll take Father down to the presbytery. Can you manage to get in on your own? Tom, wake up Tom. Can you get in on your own?'

A grunt of prehistoric eloquence presumably signified Tom's acquiescence, but the small peaceful snores had begun again as we drew up at their door. 'Oh dear. Never mind, I'll just drive you straight down Father and get Tom out somehow when I get back.'

Quite unaware of what she was saying, at that moment I slumped into semi-consciousness, and fell with my head gently cushioned on Maeve's welcoming bosom.

'There, there,' I heard her say, as she pressed me warmly into her vast embrace. Some realization of where I was must have penetrated my drink-fumed senses. I leapt up, my head striking first Maeve's jaw and then the roof of the car.

'Aargh,' I apologized. 'Oh, aargh.'

'Oh, the pair of you,' she said, feeling her jaw and obviously glad that she wasn't spitting her teeth out of the window. 'Sit up there Father, and let's get you home.'

I managed to get out of the car at the presbytery and tried

desperately to express my gratitude for such a lovely evening. Guttural noises were all I could emit. She drove off.

The moon was shining, brilliantly etching the house in magic. I used its light to look at my watch, noting with no emotion at all, that it was barely gone half past ten. I marched majestically into the house. Sadie was coming out of Father Morrison's room.

'Oh good Father,' she said. 'I've just made a cup of tea for Father. Come on into the kitchen, there's a cup left in the pot.' My march behind her was very much less than steady. The floor seemed to wobble fluidly, making my task so much more difficult.

'Have a good time then, did you Father?' She still hadn't really looked at me.

I really did try to speak. Instead I crumpled quietly onto my knees and proceeded to be sick on the floor. This brought her full attention to me. I smiled weakly in explanation.

'Dear God Father, you're as drunk as an owl. And what happened to your face, and your good suit. You look as though you've been sleeping in the bushes. Those Murphys,' she clucked. 'I'll give them a round of my tongue when I see them. But come on get upstairs. I'll clean this up. Come on.'

Poor Sadie. She dragged my helpless body into an upright position, held me as I stumbled up the stairs, helped me off with my jacket, collar and trousers and shoes, bundled me into the bed, wiped my face. I never saw the light go out, never heard her leave. A black welcoming pit enveloped me as my head hit the pillow. The room spun round just once and then gave up.

I woke in the morning with a head the size of a pumpkin. Inside an army of maniacs beat leaden gongs. My mouth was a torment of tastes and swellings. Matt McGinley's twisted prophecy seemed as though it was being fulfilled all too soon. I looked with horror into the mirror. A wild-eyed scratched savage glared back at me. With trembling hands I washed, shaved and dressed. I had to bring out my older pants. What happened to the suit I wore to the party?

Bemused, light-headed and feeling like death, I passed through the kitchen on my way to the church for morning

Mass. Sadie was there preparing Father Morrison's breakfast. He was on the early Mass that week.

'Morning, Sadie,' I mumbled.

'You're alive, are you?' she said.

'What do you mean, Sadie? What happened? Where's my suit? What time did I come in? Why do I feel so terrible?' I ended in a pathetic lament.

'Drunk, Father,' said Sadie with some relish. 'Pig-drunk. Sick all over the floor. Suit ruined. Look at your face.'

I fingered my face with nervous hands. 'Oh God Sadie, what have I done? I can't remember a thing. I went to Tom Murphy's house and after that it's all blank.' I shook my head as though to loosen memory. My eyes begged for pity.

'Well, get on into church Father,' said Sadie with apparent severity. 'We'll try to work out what happened to you later. You were a scream when you came in,' she added with a roar of laughter. 'Good job I was here.'

'Oh,' I moaned and went into church.

Tom Murphy had no more memory than I of what had happened. Maeve filled the gaps, or some of them. The rest came in shattering flashbacks over the next few days. My apologies to the Murphys and the Broadbents, delivered with shame, were uproariously rejected. It had been a very good evening. They all said so.

## CHAPTER NINE

AMID the heart-searching and remorse following upon my disgraceful performance at the Broadbents, resolutions about future behaviour emerged relentlessly. Leading the field was a determination not to mix in that society for which I was obviously unsuited. Slowly peace came back to my troubled soul, quiet too to my body, racked for days after the orgy, with spasms of sickness.

It was then with great alarm about two weeks after the party, that I answered Sadie's call, telling me I had a visitor in the waiting room. For the visitor was none other than Charlie Broadbent. A blush suffused my cheeks, my hands began to sweat.

'Hallo Father,' Charlie greeted me. 'Been to any good parties lately? Ha, ha, ha!'

I cringed, but accepted the embarrassment as fitting punishment for my excesses.

'Hallo Charlie. Has something else come up? Did I do some damage, or insult somebody?'

'Bless your soul, no Father. You're taking it all far too seriously. Nobody noticed a thing. We all go over the mark sometimes. So stop worrying about it.'

At least that was a relief. But perhaps Charlie was going to invite me to some other 'do', and after me making all those resolutions. So it was still with trepidation that I asked him, 'What can I do for you then Charlie?'

'Well it's like this Father. I've come to ask you a great favour. Both Freda and I think you're exactly the person for it. In my spare time I am a prison visitor. That may surprise you. I bet you think we just drink and enjoy ourselves all the time. But I do like to do something for disadvantaged people, so I visit prisons, see if there's any help I can give inside or out, to the prisoners appointed to my care.'

I hastily closed my mouth, and tried not to look as

astounded as I felt. Charlie Broadbent a prison visitor! That would put a bit of a spoke in Matt McGinley's wheel if he ever spoke to me again about the evil ways of the rich.

'Now, I visit both Wakefield and Galney Prisons. And in a couple of weeks one of my Galney clients is due to be released. He used to be a Catholic, I believe, which is why I thought of you.'

'But surely there's a Catholic chaplain at Galney prison? I know there is at Wakefield because I've met him. Won't he deal with any of this lad's problems?' Anxiety to help was hardly bursting out of me. But what did I know of prison or prisoners?

'Now calm down Father.' Everybody seemed obliged to say this to me. I must be giving the impression of a neurotic idiot to one and all.

'Sorry Charlie,' I said. 'Please do go on.'

'Well, this is the point Father. This is just a young lad, about twenty four (I'm only twenty five, I thought in horror). He got a ten-year sentence when he was eighteen for armed robbery. Hit someone on the head with an iron bar I believe. He's being paroled for good behaviour now. He's not an ounce of harm in him that I can see, however odd that may seem. He's just a bit lost and I thought you could help him over the first few days until he finds his feet again.'

'Is he from Brimley or something Charlie? Or has he relatives here?'

'No, no this is the point. He's from Bolton or Blackburn or somewhere but he says he has no relations at all. No one and nowhere to go to when he gets out. I asked him would he mind coming to Brimley, because I already had you in mind. You, in your business, get to know so many more people than I do, and I thought you'd be the ideal person to find him a job and a place to stay and so on. I just don't have the time you see. I do my few hours a week, and some correspondence as well, but I just would not be able to give the attention that I think this lad needs. So what about it Father? Will you give it a go? It really does need to be done, and you give me the impression that you're just the man for it.'

I was flabbergasted. How I could know what was necessary

for the aftercare of a professional hatchet-man or whatever he was? Hardened in crime, brutalized by prison. Shivers ran through me. He might do some desperate mischief to me. And I was a coward. A four-star, fully paid-up coward.

'Well Charlie, what can I say,' I finally managed to croak. 'I'm very honoured that you should think of me. But I really doubt whether I'm the man for you.'

'Look Father,' burst in Charlie, 'Why don't you just go to the prison and see him, see the warders and ask them about him, and then make up your mind. I know you'll find that there's nothing to worry about. I've fixed up an appointment for you tomorrow afternoon at three. Galney's not far away, and I'm sure you'll be able to get there.'

That was anticipation for you! I could hardly refuse. Charlie Broadbent in his different ways seemed to be a dark angel to me. My feeling of doom as he left was deep and frightening. My first problem was how to get there. As it happened Amos Greenland had been giving me driving lessons in his old jalopy. 'If you can drive this,' he had said, 'you can drive anything.'

And so it turned out. In my driving test in Barnsley the week before I had passed with flying colours, to my great surprise. So perhaps Amos would lend me his frightening vehicle for the journey to Galney. It would save so much time, and if I decided to accept the commission then it would give me a way of transporting the prisoner back. The prisoner! Dear Heaven, I didn't even know his name. Just like me to roll up to Galney and ask to see *a* prisoner. 'What, any prisoner?' the warder would say in amazement.

I hastily rang the Broadbents. Mr Charles was at the factory, some minion informed me, and very reluctantly searched out and gave me the number. After being passed from underling to underling, finally I recognized Charlie's voice.

'Broadbent here.' Very refined.

'It's me Charlie. Father Kennedy.'

'Now don't tell me you're having cold feet Father?'

'No . . . no Charlie. It just struck me that I don't know the name of your prisoner friend. Bit awkward, eh!' I brayed nervously.

'By Jove, yes,' roared Charlie. 'Terribly sorry. I never did give you his name did I? Bill Montgomery. 'Pinkie' he likes to be called, though God knows why, since he's as black as the ace of spades.'

'What . . .' I stammered. 'Do you mean he's . . . er . . . coloured? A Negro?'

'Bless my soul no!' Charlie was obviously enjoying himself. 'Very black hair, sallow skin, dark eyes. But he's from Bolton, I told you. Hardly the outposts of the Empire, eh what? Bill Pinkie Montgomery. He's all yours Father. Bye.'

He hung up. A lowering black-visaged thug materialized in my mind. Pinkie! He'd probably slaughter me if ever I dared to address him by that obviously unthuglike name. My terror redoubled. Why on earth had I ever agreed even to visit this monster? He would grab me by the throat and force me to look after him. A bit lost, said Charlie. But Charlie was a prison visitor. He would never have to see Pinkie when there were no warders to restrain him. No Pinkie would shake a ham-like fist under his nose. I reminded myself that I was over six feet. There was a lot of me however clumsily assembled. But faced with a homicidal maniac brandishing an iron bar, would not my cowardice come to full flower? Yes, yes it would. It certainly would. I shook myself and went in search of Ams.

'Course you can have t'car,' said Amos. 'I walk to t'pit. Try to keep the weight down. One of these days I'll send that cage crashing to the bottom, if I don't.'

Gratefully I explained the position to Amos.

'And I think I can help you there an' all,' he said. 'There's a vacancy coming up in just about a fortnight. On the surface, not down t'pit. Just a labourer you understand, but it'll probably suit this big fellow you're talking about. Give him time to look around if nowt else. Just leave it with me Father and I'll see t'manager and see if I can't fix it up. There's nowt he can steal there, even if he had a mind to, after all those years in prison.'

I almost jumped up and down in excited thanks. Apart

from the sheer genius of Amos in solving much of my problem, his own solid figure would always be there as counterweight to any threats issued by the dark Pinkie. I'd back Amos against anyone I had ever met. He had told me once of a friendly encounter with a judo fanatic, who seriously informed Amos that he could cope with him, twenty stone and all, as he would with a baby. 'Come on then,' Amos had said. As the expert expertly positioned himself, arms and feet at the ready, Amos quietly kicked him in the lower part of his stomach, just enough to reduce him to a groaning mass.

'They always expect you to fight by their rules,' he said to me. 'When you don't, they're completely ruined.' Oh yes, I'd back Amos even against the ferocious Pinkie.

'Another thing Father,' Amos now said to me. 'About accommodation. There's that hostel that were built years ago in Church Street, for unmarried miners coming in to t'pit. County Council have done it up again recently and it's quite nice. Why don't you go and ask them if they'd have a room for your friend? There's always people moving in and moving out.'

'Amos, you're a genius. What would I do without you? I'd never even thought about where he was going to stay. Thank you for everything.'

'Think nowt of it, lad,' said Amos.

The hostel proved to be all that Amos had forecast, and they were happy to reserve a room for Pinkie in a fortnight's time. Thanks to Amos, I now had a job, a room and transport for the bold Pinkie. All that remained was the visit.

Galney Prison from the outside is like every other prison that I had hastily passed. A huge pseudo-Norman façade, gave an imposing, if daunting dignity to the bare massive walls that spread on either side of it. The towering wooden gate studded with huge nails was further reinforced by huge bars enclosing the small inset windows. Why bother to bar the windows in the door, I wondered. Surely no escaping prisoner would be foolhardy enough to try to get out through the door? Still musing on this odd possibility I rang the ornate bell that hung to the right of the door.

A little wicket gate opened in the great door, and an impassive jailer emerged.

'Yes,' he said.

'I . . . er . . . have an appointment to see one of your . . . er . . . prisoners. Bill Montgomery? Mr Broadbent, one of your visitors, made the appointment for me. Is that alright?'

'Oh yes. You're Mr Broadbent's man are you? He said someone would be coming to see Pinkie. He likes to be called Pinkie you know. Makes him feel warm and friendly.' An empty leer flitted across his pocked face. 'Come on in then.' He stood aside to let me through, slid the heavy bolts again on the small door and took me into a small Dickensian office to the left of the gate. Inside a large sloping wooden desk added to the nineteenth-century flavour.

'Sit down there, sir, and I'll sort it out.' He pointed to a bare wooden chair. 'Funny chap, Pinkie,' he said conversationally.

My heart sank. All fears of this hulking giant returned. A shiver ran through me.

'Aye, a funny chap,' he repeated. 'Do you know, there's really only one thing a prisoner has to do for himself, and that's get up in the morning. After that, he's no choice about anything. The bell for getting up goes at seven, and twice before then, and the second bell for washing and that at half past seven, we go round each cell and rattle on the door to make sure that they're not sleeping in. The second time is about twenty five past. We go in then, and if they haven't got their feet on the floor, we kick 'em out of bed. We're not worried if they're not dressed, just so long as their feet are on the floor. Now, sir, in six whole years, Pinkie has never once had his feet on the floor! Every morning for six years we've had to kick him out of bed. He's beaten the system you know. He's never made one single decision since he came in here. I think you're going to have a bit of a rough time with him, if you're looking after him. Institutionalized. That's what they call it. And that's what he is. Or bloody lazy, if you'll excuse the word, sir.'

This was getting worse. An institutionalized thug. How on earth was I going to cope?

'Come on then sir. I'll take you through.' He sounded very cheerful. 'Then I'll bring Pinkie along and you can have a talk. Better let me know what arrangements you're making, as Pinkie'll likely forget.' He led me through two tall iron grilles which stretched from ceiling to floor in the pseudo-Norman gatehouse. At each stage the feeling of claustrophobia deepened. Even the small courtyard through which we passed to get to the main block seemed menacingly enclosed. I would die in a place like this, I thought. No criminal benefits could ever be worth the risk of ending up there.

Another door was gratingly unlocked and we proceeded down a hospital-like corridor tiled in a repulsive green. Off this opened a series of rooms into one of which my guide now showed me.

'If you just wait there, sir, I'll go and get Pinkie for you. He's on work detail just now, and since he never does anything worthwhile, he'll probably be glad to come and talk to you. I'll have to lock you in of course when he comes. Regulations you know, sir. But you'll have nothing to fear from Pinkie. And just ring that bell there when you want to come out. Right, sir?'

He went cheerily off down the corridor. Nothing to fear indeed. His merely saying that reminded me of how much fear I really had. And I was committed. Amos was looking out a job for him, and I had already booked his accommodation in the hostel. No turning back now.

The door rattled and Pinkie was ushered in. The door slammed and very obviously was locked. Pinkie sat down. He was about five feet two and very slightly built! How he could have lifted an iron bar to break somebody's skull passed comprehension. He was indeed very dark, as Charlie had said, but his face was smiling and open, and he looked scarcely eighteen.

'Hallo there . . . er . . . Bill . . . isn't it? I hear you like to be called Pinkie? Er . . . hello . . . Pinkie. I'm Father Kennedy. Your visitor, Mr Broadbent, asked me to see you and to try to fix you up when you come out.'

I proffered my hand which he shook limply.

'Mars bar,' he said. 'Mars bar. I'm going to have a Mars bar when I come out. I love Mars bars.'

'Yes, well . . . that's very nice. I . . . er . . . I've got you a job. At least I think I've got you a job. Working on the surface at the pit. Just labouring I'm afraid, but it'll give you a chance to look around.' Parotting Amos's words. 'Is there any particular type of work you like to do, and would like to look for? Perhaps I can help?'

'And chocolate toffees,' he replied. 'I love chocolate toffees too.' He nodded brightly at me.

'Very good, very good,' I said hastily, before he proffered any more of his candy fancies. 'I've got you a place to stay too. A very nice hostel where you can have your meals as well. I'll take you there when I bring you out.'

'I'm going to have a dog too. They're nice, dogs, aren't they? I've always wanted a dog.'

As a conversation it was not getting very far. But I persevered. 'I'm not sure that they'll allow dogs in the hostel, you know Pinkie. A lot of these places insist on no animals.'

'A black dog is the one I want,' he said. 'A little black dog. I don't like big dogs. One bit me once.' The memory creased his face in a scowl, which seemed to indicate that if there were a big dog around, and he had his iron bar, he would do terrible deeds to the animal.

I tried again. 'I'll come and pick you up and bring you to Brimley. Eight o'clock isn't it, when they . . . er . . . let . . . er open the gates?'

'Fishing too,' he informed me. 'I've always thought I'd like to do a bit of fishing.' The scowl was gone, happiness restored to his childlike face.

I gave up. 'Well, that's great Pinkie,' I said. 'I'll collect you. You'll be ready eh? Ha! ha! And I'll take you to your hostel and show you where to start work the following day.'

'Biscuits,' he vouchsafed. 'Biscuits are nice.'

I rang the bell. 'Goodbye then Pinkie. See you in a fortnight.'

'Chocolate biscuits,' he was saying as the door opened.

I checked with the warder as I left, the day and the hour of his departure. I was strongly tempted to say 'Mars bar'. He had me as daft as he was.

Occasionally during the next fortnight I managed to put Pinkie out of my head. But most of the time he hung there like a black cloud. How would he possibly cope with the world, lost as he was in a maze of Mars bars, biscuits and dogs? The tremors of physical fears had passed to be replaced by a growing sense of anxiety about Pinkie's place in the world. Nonetheless, I confirmed his booking in the hostel, and even paid his first week's dues. And Amos assured me that the labouring job was his and that no embarrassing questions would be asked. Things should work out.

But in spite of the bright glory of the morning and the warming certainty that I had done everything that could be done, my journey to Galney in Amos's car was filled with dark forebodings. The sunlight emphasized if anything the gloom of the prison, but Pinkie, as he came out to me, looked back as though leaving a loved home. He was neatly dressed in his clothes of six years ago, and carried a small pathetic brown-paper parcel of all the rest of his worldly goods.

'Well, that's that Pinkie, eh? Never back there again? A new start, new home, new job. I've arranged with our housekeeper to give you breakfast. I'm sure the food in . . . er . . . there, is not the best in the world. And then I'll show you your hostel and the pit where you'll begin tomorrow. And thank God you've got a nice day to begin. Everything looks better on a nice day doesn't it?'

'Whippets,' he said. 'Changed my mind. I'm going to have a whippet.'

Since many of the miners kept, trained and raced whippets, I thought that at least, this once, he was making a connection. A mining community, need to fit in, have a whippet.

'Very good,' I said in delight.

'Bones,' he continued. 'Need to give them bones.'

'Yes, yes of course. You can buy bones in the butcher's for next to nothing. We do. We have a dog, Jasper, and we buy bones. He's a big dog though, I don't think you'd like him.'

I had left very careful instructions that Jasper was not to be in evidence when I brought Pinkie in. Jasper had become devoted to me and followed me on my rounds. But he might frighten Pinkie, especially after the 'big dog' revelation of a fortnight ago.

'Bolton,' he said shattering any illusions of consecutive thought. 'Nice place Bolton.'

Despite my bewilderment at these constant switches, I seemed to recognize Bolton. Wasn't that where Charlie had told me that Pinkie was born? Yes, I was sure it was Bolton. Undaunted then, I persisted. 'Oh yes Bolton. Isn't that where you were born?'

'Railways,' was the answer. 'Used to like looking at railways.'

Despair filled me. I passed the twenty minutes back to Brimley with spasmodic comments on the local scenery or lack of it, ignoring all the inconsequential remarks that emerged in a kind of insane parlour game, from Pinkie's subconscious.

The breakfast prepared by Sadie and lovingly laid out, he devoured like a wolf. Never a word of praise or thanks. When the last morsel had been wiped from his plate, he merely looked up with a sweet smile as though to say, 'What's next on the programme?'

By lunch-time when I had taken him to his hostel, introduced him to the manager at the pit, and acted as his interpreter in accepting the job, and returned him to his hostel for lunch, I was exhausted. After eating I sat in my armchair virtuously tired and dozed off.

I roused myself at about three o'clock to continue my normal work. Pinkie had been dominating my life, and I felt that I had been neglecting my more permanent people. I walked out the door to move to my district and fell sprawling over the figure of Pinkie seated on the doorstep.

'Biscuits,' he said in some pain. 'Chocolate biscuits.'

Gathering his crumpled frame from the ground he reached into his pocket for a packet of now broken biscuits. Dazed, I accepted one. No attempt at conversation did I make. Resignedly I set my face towards his hostel and Pinkie followed in my wake, only a slight variation on Jasper who had given me up this past few days.

'Now don't come to the presbytery again today Pinkie,' I said as I led him into the hostel. 'I'm very busy tonight, and I really won't have time to see you. But I'll come round tomorrow evening after you come back from work and see how you're doing. So good luck tomorrow. It must be a good feeling to be going to your first real job in so long?' Pinkie looked very dubious, but rather heroically proffered me another biscuit.

'I like chocolate biscuits,' was his farewell. Almost a lament.

Doom fell at eleven the next morning. First the telephone from the pit. The irate manager informed me that Pinkie had never arrived. Reproachfully he told me that he had no choice but to ask another man who was also looking for a job, to take the position. My apologies were embarrassed, almost tearful. Where on earth would I get Pinkie another job? Why wasn't he there?

It hit me like a thunderbolt. He was still in bed of course. After years of being kicked out of bed he wouldn't know how to get out himself. I grabbed my coat, rushed for the door. Standing at the door, his hand about to ring the bell was a large police sergeant.

'Ah, good morning, sir,' he intoned. 'You wouldn't be Father Kennedy would you?' I indicated that I was and said that I was in a hurry on a somewhat urgent case.

'Won't keep you long Father. May I just step inside?'

'I'm very sorry, Sergeant. I've lost all my manners this morning. Do come in please. I'm in a bit of a state.' I led him into the waiting room.

'Well Father,' he said ponderously. 'We have information that you received a Bill Pinkie Montgomery from Galney gaol yesterday.'

I nodded speechlessly. What could have happened to poor Pinkie.

'We had to pick him up again this morning, here in the main street, and he's in Wakefield gaol waiting to come before the magistrates tomorrow.'

'Oh dear,' I sighed, feeling vaguely that I had let him down. Perhaps I should have seen him again the night before. 'What did he do?'

'Well,' said the sergeant, 'it was all a bit odd. He waited outside a sweet shop until a delivery van drove up. As the driver unlocked the van and took a consignment into the shop, he apparently stepped into the van, took out a box of sweets and tried to sell them to passers-by just there. He didn't even move away or run or anything. Almost as if he wanted to be caught.'

He did, of course. Want to be caught, I mean. He wanted to go back to his home, where no decisions ever had to be taken.

'Was it a box of Mars bars?' I asked weakly.

'How did you guess Father? Will you be wanting to see him? I could lay on a car to take you to Wakefield.'

'I don't think so Sergeant. I think it would be a waste of time. There's nothing I can do for him. He's back where he wants to be. Institutionalized, the warder said. That's Pinkie, and from the look of him, that will always be Pinkie.'

'Right oh then Father. I thought we'd better let you know. Sorry to have kept you from your urgent case.'

'That's alright Sergeant. Pinkie *was* my urgent case.'

# CHAPTER TEN

THE conclusion of my ill-fated adventures with Pinkie left me numb but relieved. It was with gratitude that I returned to the ordinary routine of the parish. Nobody reproached me for my failure, not Father Morrison nor Charlie Broadbent. They were much more aware than was I that human affairs rarely follow the pattern of logic or good sense. Only I saw in my failure a source of shame, but it too began to fade against the continuous flow of work and experience which any parish provides.

One of the chores which I found particularly demanding was school visiting. After our first visit together and its culmination in the confessional, Father Morrison left me to make my own arrangements with the head and the teachers. Regularly as I went in, I always found it very difficult to make contact with the children. They sat polite and wide-eyed, but my feeble attempts at jokes were completely beyond them. I seemed to finish every visit in red-faced confusion.

'Don't worry about it Father,' Father Morrison used to encourage me. 'Children are the most difficult audience in the world. You ask any comedian. The only way to get them is to pretend to be as young as they are. They know you're pretending, and hopefully so do you, and somehow they like it, and will laugh with you. I'm no one to teach you. I'm not much good at it myself, but they're used to me and humour me. But above all, don't get flustered about it. It makes them very uneasy to see an insecure adult. They expect all adults to be sure. Some they like, some they don't, but they don't know how to react at all to uncertainty. Just keep at it, you'll be alright.'

So I kept at it, but with no measurable improvement. Thus every Tuesday morning I steeled myself and went in for morning prayers and the first half hour. I went early and had to pass through the milling playground. Some of the children used to crowd around me, especially the younger girls. 'Good morning Father,' they would chant, and hanging on to my arms and coat would escort me proudly to the door. Why weren't they as responsive in the classroom, I used to wonder. It had to be me and my mouth, which reduced them from such spontaneous friendliness to wide-eyed stupefaction. They were ready enough to be entertained. I just couldn't do it.

This particular Tuesday nobody came to grab my hand or to intone the usual 'Good morning Father'. It wasn't, I soon discovered, that they had come to a communal decision to ignore me. There was just a far better diversion going on in a corner of the playground and they were all crowding around, for all the world like a swarm of bees. Knowing that children's diversions are often full of menace for somebody, I decided to investigate. Even from my lofty point of view it was impossible to discern what attraction lay in the middle of the crowd until I was actually among them, almost treading on them as they completely ignored my presence.

There in the middle, rolling around on the hard playground, was a whirl of figures. It wasn't until I actually pulled apart the bodies pounding and pulling at each other, that I found there were three of them. Only one of them did I recognize as I held them apart, two with my arms, one with my knee. The one circling around my knee, blind to all but his own fury, blind even to who I was, was Willie, the famous Willie who had made such a lasting impression on my first visit to the school.

'Willie, Willie,' I shouted. 'What on earth is all this about? Who are these two boys and what are you all fighting about? Come on, come on, it's all over now.'

Willie shook the glaze from his eyes, looked up at me with some surprise, gulped and began to look ashamed.

I turned to the buzzing crowd. 'Come on now children, it's all over. Off you go and play.'

Obediently, if reluctantly, they began to drift to other parts of the playground. A good fight was obviously much better fun than playing hopscotch, tig, skipping, or whatever other pastime occupied them in the space before they had to conform to school discipline. As they moved away I was able to look more closely at my three combatants. Willie looked just the same as he always did, unwashed, torn jumper, uncombed and generally dishevelled. Poor Willie. I had visited his home, and seen his friendly but incapable family, and knew that little or nothing could be done to improve Willie's appearance.

The other two were in exact contrast to Willie. Though they too were at that moment somewhat grubby and disordered, this was but a temporary veneer. Their clothes were well cared for, their hair neatly cut, their general appearance betokening a very different background to that of Willie. Perhaps he was attacking them precisely because they were so different.

'What's your name?' I said to the blond cherubic one with the blue eyes, who dangled from my right hand.

'Gregory, Father. Gregory O'Keefe.' His voice was nicely modulated, despite the barely restrained anger that thickened it.

'And yours?' I turned to the child on my left. His hair was black and straight, his face had a tinge of olive, his eyes were a deep impenetrable brown.

'Daniel,' he said. 'Daniel Lercaro, Father.' His manners reasserted themselves. I knew neither of them.

'Are you from Brimley?' I asked.

'Yes Father,' they replied.

'We're both new here Father,' said Daniel, casting a look of venom at Gregory.

'Well, this won't do will it?' I said with hearty cheerfulness. 'What's it all about, eh?' Neither Daniel nor Gregory raised eyes or voice.

'Miss, Miss,' pleaded Willie, in his usual confusion as to the sex of authority. 'Miss, they was fighting. Horribly,' he added rolling his eyes. 'And I were just trying to stop 'em. Honest I was Miss. I don't know why they was fighting.'

As I was about to follow up this astonishing piece of information, the bell rang. I would never find out whether Willie was indeed taking an unlikely role as peacemaker. Willie loved fighting just for its own sake. He had no fear, and never held any grudges against anybody whose eye he might black or whose nose he might bloody.

'Alright then,' I said. 'Now run off and don't let's see you fighting any more.'

I followed them into the school for my own particular purgatory of leading the morning prayers and then having a talk with one of the classes. Quite by accident the class I was due for that particular morning was the one which included Willie, Daniel and Gregory. During my even less than usually successful attempts to rouse them to religious fervour, I was aware ever and anon of Willie's, Daniel's and Gregory's eyes fixed on me. There seemed to be apprehension, perhaps lest I inform on them. When I finally then had enough and bade them all good morning, I carefully avoided having any words with Miss Laverty, their elderly teacher, as I would normally have done. They must see that I wasn't going to get them into trouble. Somebody I'm sure would split to the teacher. Children are notoriously unfaithful to their friends. But it wasn't going to be me.

Willie's version of affairs did however intrigue me, so I went to the headmistress, the same Sister Clare who had officiated at my first introduction to the school. 'Sister,' I said, 'I'm not reporting anybody or asking that they be punished, but I would really like to know what was going on.' I gave her the story of the early morning fight, including Willie's version of affairs, and asked could she shed any light on the matter.

'Well Father, obviously I can't be sure because I didn't see it happen, but if I were a betting nun, I'd lay a little wager that Willie was telling the truth. Don't look so surprised Father. Whatever else about Willie, and there's a lot else, I've never known him speak anything but the truth. Even if he's found out in the most terrible things he always admits whatever he has done.' That was a nice little testimonial to Willie. The mind boggled at what Sister Clare in her gentle innocence considered 'terrible things'.

'And the other two boys, Gregory and Daniel, are both rather disturbed children. They're both new to the school just this last couple of weeks Father, though there's no connection between their families. As you can see they're from what are popularly called 'good homes'. Gregory's parents have split up. He lives with his mother and as far as I can gather, sees his father at weekends. He's with another woman.' She sniffed disapprovingly. 'So it's probably the disturbance of that, which has made him a very touchy child. He won't talk about his father at all. He even pretends, I gather, to some of the children that his father is just working away. I heard him quite by accident one day telling another child that his father was dead! So there's obviously upset there, and possibly Daniel taunted him about his father. Children do you know Father. They can be awfully cruel.'

It had been one of my more painful discoveries this past few months to see examples of this. Lurking so often behind the beautiful innocent exterior of so many children, was a degree of calculated cruelty that would be hard to match in any but the most criminal adult. I nodded sympathetically to Sister Clare.

'But you said Daniel was also a . . . er . . . disturbed child, Sister. Is he from the same kind of background?'

'No Father,' she said, 'that's the surprising thing. Daniel's father and mother have four or five children, all older than Daniel, and are pillars of the community. I don't really know what's wrong with him. Such a good home. Perhaps being the youngest he's been spoilt too much. But that wouldn't seem to me to explain his very odd attitude. Perhaps he's just the bad apple in the bunch?' she finished lamely.

'I'll tell you what Sister. Since they're new to the parish and I didn't even know about them, I'll get their addresses from you and go to visit them in the normal way. I'll leave it a few days in case either Daniel or Gregory thinks I'm telling tales on them, and I'd be very grateful if you did nothing about it at your end for the same reason. Perhaps if they trust me I may be able to help a bit more.'

She assured me that she would do nothing, and I left. She was a good-hearted soul. Perhaps her fears were exaggerated. I went about my business for the next few days, and indeed it was over a week before I remembered and had the opportunity to visit the O'Keefe and Lercaro families.

Mrs O'Keefe had taken a house up on the hill. Though rather more modest, than say the Murphys' or the Broadbents', it was still a gracious and beautifully furnished home. Mrs O'Keefe fairly obviously lacked for nothing. She was a tall, very thin lady, her face wrinkled, as are those of many very thin people, giving an impression that she was older than I'm sure she was. I estimated her age at about forty.

'Come in Father,' she greeted me effusively, though the smile which wreathed her face, seemed not to touch her eyes at all. Just the externals of courtesy I thought, though it was rather a shivery experience.

'I just found out about your being here, with Gregory coming to the school.' My nervousness was normal. I'm sure she put me down as a gauche country boy. At that moment, Gregory himself came into the room where I was sitting with his mother. Everything was so meticulously placed and polished that I sat edgily on an obviously expensive chair. He looked at me inscrutably.

'Oh yes, Gregory. Come and meet Father . . . Kennedy is it?' I nodded dumbly. 'Poor Gregory, he's so upset. His father left us you know. We came here because my sister lives here. Mrs Jordan, do you know her?'

'I know of her, Mrs O'Keefe,' I replied. She was one of the Broadbent circle, lived further up the hill. She'd been at that dreadful party, I suddenly remembered.

'She's not a Catholic though, is she Mrs O'Keefe?' I shot the words out rapidly and knew I was blushing.

'No, no Father, don't worry. You've not been neglecting your duties.' She smiled that hollow smile again. 'I'm a convert. I became a Catholic for Gregory's father. It's even more terrible that he should leave us. I mean it's a sin for a Catholic, isn't it Father?'

She didn't wait for a reply. Her arm was still around Gregory who stood frighteningly still.

'Poor Gregory,' she repeated. 'You know when he told us, Mr O'Keefe I mean, that he was leaving us for that other hussy, Gregory cried and cried. I want a daddy, he kept saying. Poor Gregory..' She crooned over him. I coughed.

'I think it would be better if Gregory went to play while we talk grown-up talk.' I smiled at the poor lad. 'Don't you think so Mrs O'Keefe?'

'Oh, Gregory knows all about it. I think it's better for a child to be told things don't you Father?'

'Well . . . er . . . yes, I suppose so. But if not for Gregory's sake, please let him go and play for my sake. I'm not very good with children, as Gregory knows, don't you Gregory?' I smiled hideously and beseechingly at him.

'Oh very well,' she said with obvious reluctance. 'Off you go then Gregory dear, while Father and I talk.'

He went out of the room. He looked shrunken, the skin stretched across the bones of his face. He had said not a single word.

'It's awfully cruel of a father to leave a child. To leave a wife as well. What am I going to do for the rest of my life? I'm not at all well you know Father. I suffer terribly with my nerves. He lives in Sheffield with that new woman of his. She's younger of course. That's all it is you know Father. Just a silly middle-aged attempt to get back his youth. I still love him of course. I want him to come back for Gregory's and my sake. He does need a daddy you know.'

'Well, at least he seems to have left you well provided for.' I looked round the opulent furnishings of the room and smiled embarrassedly.

'I wasn't going to leave all my furniture to that creature,' she said. 'And of course he's got to provide for his wife and son. That's the law, isn't it Father?'

'Do you have a job yourself?' I asked hopefully, thinking that the conversation might take a less personal tone.

'Oh no Father. I'm far too ill. And I've never worked you know. He'll just have to keep us. And that's quite right, isn't it Father? If only he'd come back he'd be saved all that expense. Father,' as if struck by a brilliant idea, 'why don't you go and see him and persuade him to come back. You know Gregory and now you know me. You could tell him how awful it is, how much we miss him and need him. Would you Father? Would you please?' Her voice broke in a sob.

'Don't cry Mrs O'Keefe. Please. Yes. I'll go and see him if you want. Sure I will. I'm not very good with people, but maybe he's just wanting someone to push him a little. I'm sure he'll want to do the best thing for Gregory. I'm sure he'll come back.'

'Oh you're so good Father,' she cried. 'Gregory, Gregory.'

Gregory bounded back into the room at the anguished call of his mother. 'Father's going to see your Daddy and ask him to come back to us. Isn't that wonderful. Maybe he'll be back very soon.'

Gregory stood in that frightening stillness he had shown earlier. No smile lit his face, no word escaped his lips. It was eerie. I hastily excused myself, got the address of Mr O'Keefe in Sheffield and left the house assuring Mrs O'Keefe that I'd let her know what happened. Gregory just looked.

My amazement had eased by supper time and I told Father Morrison of my experiences, and my intended visit to the Lercaros.

'I can solve your problem with the Lercaros,' he said to my surprise.

'I visited them almost as soon as they arrived. I had a letter about them from a parish priest in Blackpool. That's where they were before they came here. Very sad and nothing anybody can do. They hate each other, simple as that. They're staying together just for the children and all the children are very peculiar. So would you be if you lived in a house where hate is the dominant emotion. The eldest girl who's only sixteen has already had an abortion. With any other family she'd have been taken into care, but they have so much money, they can cover it up. The next two boys have been in the hands of the police – stealing I think. One's still on probation. And Daniel from what I gather, seems to be going the same way. What can we do Father? They're following all the rules, not breaking up the marriage, giving the children a "good home", no divorce. And in so doing they are steadily destroying all their children. Makes you wonder if the books are always right, doesn't it?' He looked at me quizzically. I was appalled.

'You're not suggesting they should divorce, are you Father?'

'Well it makes you think, as I say. They couldn't be doing

the children any more harm. They might even have a chance of being reasonably stable if that terrible atmosphere were taken away from them. You could feel it you know Father. Everyone was so polite, everything seemed so ordinary on the surface. Nothing was said about the situation by either them or me. But you could feel it,' he repeated.

I was bewildered. 'But it's not like that with the O'Keefe's Father. Just the opposite. She wants him to come back and make the home happy again. It's sadness that has disturbed Gregory, not hate.'

'Well wait and see Father,' counselled Father Morrison. 'There's always another side to every story you hear. Never make a judgement, till you've heard all sides.'

I went to bed that night in a very disturbed frame of mind. The teaching on marriage, it's sanctity and permanence, seemed to have taken a few hard knocks. My dreams were shot through with O'Keefes and Lercaros locked in battle on the dusty surface of the school playground.

During the next few days I made several attempts to telephone Mr O'Keefe but it wasn't until over a week after my visit to Gregory's mother that the phone was finally answered.

'O'Keefe,' said an abrupt voice.

'Ah. Good evening Mr O'Keefe. You won't know me. Father Kennedy from Brimley, St Aloysius, where your wife and son live now.'

There was an ominous silence from the other end of the phone. I rushed on. 'Would it be possible for me to come to see you some time? Anytime that suits you.'

'You're most welcome to come any time Father. I presume you've got the address. Do you know where it is?'

'Yes, yes, thank you Mr O'Keefe.' Relief flooded my voice.

'Well then, would tomorrow night suit you? Say about eight? I can't think what you want to see me about, or perhaps I can, come to that. You've been to the house in Brimley, you say? Come anyway. Good night Father.'

A very self-possessed, very abrupt man was Mr O'Keefe. My satisfaction at having finally made contact began to shade into my usual nervousness. What if I made a mess of the interview, as was so likely, and spoilt forever what chance there was of Gregory being reunited with his father? Life was so complicated and I was so clumsy. Another disturbed night tormented me.

Poor Amos willingly lent me his car again, with strict, if mocking, injunctions not to drink. He'd heard in the usual grapevine fashion of my performance at the Broadbents'! I assured him that with or without his warnings, I would not be so foolish as to drink while in charge of a car. I even declared that I would never drink again, that I had withdrawn my mental reservation to the Lord. Amos smiled his slow smile and bade me bon voyage.

The address in Sheffield turned out to be a solid Victorian stone house which had been converted into flats. Mr O'Keefe had the upper one. He came to the door himself in answer to my ring. My own height, with short cropped hair grizzling at the temples, he was by any standards a startingly handsome man. Inside the cosy warmth of the living-room he introduced me to a tall brunette. That she was wearing heavy black glasses, presumably for reading, as she took them off as she shook my hand, detracted not at all from the classic high cheek-boned beauty of her face. She was indeed considerably younger than Mr O'Keefe, although as the evening went on, this age gap was clearly no barrier to the affection between them.

'This is Anne, Father. You'll have heard of Anne of course.'

'Good evening Father.' A warm low voice, no embarrassment.

'Drink, Father?' said Mr O'Keefe.

'No . . . no thanks Mr O'Keefe. No. I had a very unfortunate experience with drink a little while ago and I'd prefer not to risk it again, especially as I'm driving.'

'Right then. Well, do sit down Father. And please call me Declan. That's my name. Mr O'Keefe sounds terribly formal. And as you can see we're not terribly formal.'

They were both dressed in loose-fitting sweaters and

casual trousers and indeed looked far too comfortable to be formal. The room too had none of the almost neurotic neatness that had characterized the O'Keefe house in Brimley. It was lived-in, a room of ease and relaxation.

'Now,' said Mr O'Keefe, Declan, 'what can we do for you?'

'I've come to ask you to go back to your wife and child . . . Mr . . . er . . . Declan. They miss you and need you so much.' I gabbled the words. My usual calm mature diplomacy. I added a ghastly grin of apology towards Anne. To my consternation they burst into loud and quite genuine laughter.

'She really did take you in Father. I've no doubt she told you how she loved me? I'll bet she had Gregory there too, quivering with fear? Mention her nerves? Now listen Father, I have no doubt you came here in good faith, to restore a man to the bosom of his family. But there's a lot she didn't tell you as well. She didn't tell you that I'd been back twice since I first left, and that each time she drove me out with a venom and a savagery that you can't even imagine. That she has systematically tried to poison Gregory's mind against me. That it was she who insisted on telling Gregory that I was leaving, and telling him in the most savage and obscene way she could devise. That time and again she waits until he's just about to come for a weekend with us, and then throws one of her nerve-tantrums and forces him to stay and look after her. That she's been to this very house and assaulted Anne.' He paused, breathing heavily. I sat absolutely still. 'That is an evil woman Father. I know an awful lot of blame attaches to me, for falling in love with Anne and leaving in the first place. But I did try to put it right – twice. And you can imagine, or maybe as a priest you can't, what that did to Anne. It's a miracle she ever put up with me. I love Gregory, more than most fathers I know love their sons. But to try to go on living with that woman to give him a full home would be to destroy him even more than this way. I'm only sorry that he's with her. But I felt so guilty that I couldn't take him away, and now she's sucking the life from him. You can see him come alive when he comes here, where there's no hate, where no one tries to poison his mind even against her.' He paused again. Anne was sitting in complete repose, and even I insensitive as I was, could feel the warmth and comfort of her love reaching out to him.

'I know you'll say that marriage is a sacrament. For better and for worse. That the child is the first consideration. But do you honestly think that a child benefits from living in a house of hate?' Father Morrison's words came back to me. Here in reverse was the exact position.

'I'm very sorry I disturbed you. Disturbed you both,' I said humbly. 'I really didn't know the situation. Please forgive my clumsiness.' We chatted a while and I left. I chose an afternoon when I knew Gregory would be at school to tell Mrs O'Keefe that her husband would not be coming back. I listened to her vituperation and hadn't the courage to challenge her version. It was so ingrained now that no one, and especially not I, could shake her conviction of her own righteousness. The next time I went into the school Gregory shyly came over to me as I crossed the playground. Before the gang of girls could lay hands on me, he spoke to me quietly.

'Did you like my dad, Father?'

'Yes I did Gregory. I liked him very much,' I said with a catch in my voice.

'Thank you Father,' he said and moved away again. Gregory was going to survive I thought as I brushed the tears from my eyes. But what about poor Daniel? I went in for my weekly agony.

## CHAPTER ELEVEN

As the days lengthened into summer. Father Morrison kept asking me when I would be taking my holidays. With the silly and ultimately selfish conviction that there were too many things that needed to be seen through before I could be spared, I kept deferring the decision.

'Look Father,' said Father Morrison one night after supper, 'you are going to have to make up your mind. I've told you that I'm going only in late September and I've already arranged a supply priest for the weekends for that time. But if you don't hurry up, I'm not going to be able to get anyone when you do eventually decide that the parish can live without you.'

'I really am sorry Father. Just because it will take me no time at all to arrange my holiday in Ireland, I've never stopped to think of your problem in getting a supply. Right then, I'll go in August if that suits you, and that will give me plenty of time to pick up the pieces before you go away. I'm sorry Father.'

And so it was arranged. All I had to do was to write to my cousins in Galway to ask if I might stay with them again, as I had now for so many years. Being farmers, they never went on formal holidays. Indeed holidays have never been a practice for country folk. Perhaps they are right. Perhaps this conviction that we have to 'get away from it all' is part of, if not the creator of, the very 'work' neurosis which gives rise to the need for holidays. The rich and leisured who really invented holidays, never pretended any justification for their jaunts. They just enjoyed them. We are loathe to admit that we just wish to enjoy ourselves, hence we create the myth of being worn out by work. The holiday then is therapeutic and not merely enjoyment. For whatever reason anyway, I was to go on holiday in August.

Assiduously I made sure in the preceding weeks that I visited and attended to all my old and sick, and even my problem people. I had been vainly trying to deal with their problems for the best part of a year, so that it was unlikely that I would come up with some magical solution just before I went away. I visited them anyway. I marvelled again at how little I had known when I first came to Brimley, at how many mistakes I had made, how many failures I had chalked up. Surely no priest ever had stumbled so frequently in the sacred aisles. And still I knew so little. So many areas of life and behaviour seemed quite beyond my capacity. At least when I returned to Brimley this time, I would not be quite as naïve as I had been a year before.

I spent the Sunday with my parents in Kingsmill and on the Monday took the train to Holyhead, and crossed by the night ferry to Ireland. I said my Mass in the pro-Cathedral in Dublin, where half the priests in the world seemed to be gathered to say Mass, and walked down the lovely wide pavements of O'Connell Street to Wynn's Hotel where I had breakfast. I had booked a hire-car and arranged for the firm to deliver it to me at Wynn's. This was rather presumptuous of me, as the only car I had ever driven was Amos's. He had said that if I could drive that, I could drive anything, so I hoped he was right.

Duly at 10 o'clock, I was paged and went to meet the respresentative of the car-hire firm in the lounge. We filled up all the papers, I payed my dues, and he slapped the car keys into my hand.

'Good luck Father,' he said. 'Have a good holiday.'

With my usual lack of organized thought, I realized when he had gone, that I had not asked him to explain to me the workings of the car. Surely it would be straightforward. Wouldn't it? I picked up my case, walked out to the car. There it stood gleaming and new. When I opened the door it had that elusive car smell. I think they must spray it into new cars. I deposited my case in the back, sat down proudly behind the wheel.

The first problem was to find the ignition. Nothing on the dashboard. Nothing on the ledges below it. I began to panic, and as I rolled my eyes frantically around the car to find somewhere, anywhere, into which I could insert my key, quite by accident I came across the fitting in the steering column. My heart was already beating far too fast as I inserted the key, and heard the engine catch sweetly, warmly, and first time.

I steadied myself, looked up and down the road to see that all was clear, and prepared to pull out and drive off. Dear Heaven, which was first gear?

There was no little diagram on the gear-lever, no indication anywhere on the dashboard as to the order of gears. Even if I found first gear, how would I ever know where reverse was? And me in the middle of Dublin and facing away from O'Connell Street, and hence in the wrong direction for where I wished to head. Memories of Amos's gear lever came back to me. First gear must be left and up. Gingerly I fitted it in, released the brake and slowly let in the clutch. The car leapt as if shot, and leapt backwards. Fortunately there was nothing behind me. At least I knew now where reverse was. I fiddled again, released the clutch with delicate tenderness, and this time moved forward chugging like an ancient tractor. I must have been in third gear, but I was moving and that was a triumph.

By the time I had cleared, after many a wrong turning, the outskirts of Dublin and was on my way west, I had mastered the gears and even come to terms with the ferocious clutch. I felt years older. The road across Ireland is flat, uninteresting and, more often than not, raised above the bog-land, so that frighteningly deep ditches plunge to either side of it. Irish drivers are most courteous. As they dawdle along about their country business they go to great lengths to wave you past as you speed more urgently along. The only problem is that they concentrate so much on their waving arm and desire to see you on your way, that they temporarily take their attention from the essential business of steering. Several times in that my first drive across the hinterland of Ireland, I found my courteous countrymen veering gently across the road as they beckoned me on, and very nearly driving me into the ditch on the wrong side of the road.

My cousins lived on a small farm just east of Galway City. Galway City is an odd phrase, as the place appears to be not much more than an overgrown village with all the happy friendliness that characterizes villages. There is great rivalry in Ireland as to which region is the most hospitable, but in my limited experience I have to give the palm to Galway. The soft gentleness of their accent is reflected in the open unquestioning delight of the people in making you welcome.

My cousins were quietly pleased that I had brought a car. They were still at the pony and trap stage, and there are limitations in that form of transport. But the first job was to go to the local village to arrange with the parish priest about saying Mass. He was an odd character, nervous as a skittery pony, his deep sonorous voice quite ruined by a desperate stammer. My cousin Jack, a rough and ready farmer of some sixty years, had always displayed towards him that quivering awe so common among Irish people in their relationship with their priests. But come hell or high water Jack insisted on coming down with me. Hospitality demanded it.

'H. . . h . . . hello Father. Father D . . . Dermot isn't it,' said Father Cashman the parish priest as we were greeted at his door. 'C . . . come in. You t . . . too, Jack.'

Jack almost literally touched his forlock as we entered. He held his hat in a reverential pose somewhere between his legs. We sat in the priest's study.

'I'd just like to make arrangements about saying Mass while I'm here Father.' I was much more self-possessed than I had been a year before, when my own newly-ordained nervousness outmatched that of Father Cashman.

'Certainly, certainly. We'll f . . . f . . . fix whatever time, s . . . suits you. Now what about a c . . . cup of c . . . coffee?'

'That's most kind of you Father,' I said.

Jack rather brusquely refused, and as soon as Father Cashman was out of the room to organize the coffee, he turned to me with some asperity.

'What the hell did you take coffee for?' he said. 'If you'd refused he'd have offered us a whisky for sure. You're still a bit of an eejut, aren't you?'

He smiled. I marvelled. Not only had I grown up in the

past year but Jack had grown beyond me. Such temerity of thought would have been unthinkable a year before. His hopes were not in vain either, as Father Cashman, on returning with a solitary cup of coffee for me, turned to Jack and said, 'I'm sure a wee drop of the c . . . cratur would be better for the likes of us Jack. You'll have one?'

I never did find out what had brought about the change in Jack, but it certainly seemed to be reflected in other people in the country as well. A healthy upsurge of anti-clericalism perhaps, or, at the very least, the beginning of a recognition that priests were only human beings like everyone else. There had been too much clerical tyranny in Ireland for far too long.

So I was not so surprised when I met the attitude again, though it was a different and less friendly kind of reaction. I took various of the relatives to different places for the day, Clifden, Sligo, Achill Island, Ennis, a roster of names that conveys nothing of the wild beauty and unspoilt character of so much of the west of Ireland. And we decided to spend a couple of days in Cork, again with relatives. It was too far to drive comfortably there and back in the one day.

Thus it was that Jack and myself were walking at lunchtime down the little cul-de-sac in Cork that leads to the Oyster Bar, whose food is famous the world over. Some few yards ahead of us two men, obviously drunk, were having a violent argument. The language and oaths were hair-raising. One of the two, possibly less drunk than the other, saw us out of the corner of his eyes.

'Whisht Pat,' I heard him say. 'Watch the language, there's a priest coming.'

Pat turned owlishly towards us and with a speed worthy of a striking rattlesnake, reached his hand into his pocket and withdrew a bread-bun, which he hurled with great force at his long-suffering companion.

'Damn you,' he shouted at him. 'And damn the Pope too,' turning with great venom towards us. He hitched up his shoulders and stumbled back into the pub which he had obviously just left. The other wee man rolled his eyes at me, shrugged his shoulders and walked away. Jack seemed not the slightest bit non-plussed by this evidence of anti-clericalism, though I suspect if he'd been in range he'd have hit the fellow just for insulting me. I was his cousin after all, never mind the priest bit.

But the weeks in Ireland were far too full of simple enjoyment for me to be perturbed by little incidents of this kind, and as I said, I was beginning to have some sympathy for the attitude anyway. And the priests seemed to be accepting it in good part and even changing to more liberal attitudes themselves. One of the local curates near Galway had even taken to training and racing greyhounds, which made him popular with many of the younger men in the district, including Michael, Jack's son, and my second cousin therefore. They were all very precise about these degrees of kinship.

'Father Collins is great,' said Michael to me one day. 'You know how it is with greyhounds Dermot, you get the odds on them at the track, according to the speed they've clocked in their previous few outings. So when you really want to win a race, and get decent odds too, all you do is feed up the beast just before his few previous races. He runs slowly, because his belly's full of food, and they don't think much of him. Then you starve him before the real race, and he goes like a bullet after the hare, and you land a nice little sum.' I had never known there was so much to greyhound racing.

'Anyway,' he said, 'I got a bit worried about this one time. It seemed like cheating, you know. So when I was at confession one Saturday – I always go to Father Collins – I said to him that I'd been doing this with the dogs. "Yerra that's no sin," says he to me. "Don't we all do that." I tell you Dermot there's a priest in a million.'

For once I didn't try to examine the theology of that opinion. I just joined in the laughter. Michael was as happily religious as anybody had any right to be. So why should I pedantically argue about the rights and wrongs of overfeeding greyhounds. I'm sure the hounds themselves had no complaints, whatever about the punters.

But whatever variations of thought there were about the Ten Commandments, they were as nothing compared to the attitudes towards the law of the land. There was a wild anarchy abroad in Ireland which defied any logic. The law that nobody either knew or cared about, from De Valera on down, was the law about drinking on Sundays. It didn't worry me, as after the debacle at the Broadbent's, I was still very much on the waggon. A few bottles of stout were all that passed my lips, and that in Ireland is asceticism of a high order. My cousins, though they drank rarely, believed in having a real go whenever they did. And this meant on every outing we had.

I was driving them down to Limerick one Sunday for a game of Irish football, always played on a Sunday. We were passing through some small village about one o'clock, nearer to Limerick than Galway, when up pipes Michael.

'Slow down now Dermot, and we'll have a wee drink here before we go on to the match. Warms the heart you know, and improves the voice for shouting.'

'Good idea boy,' said Jack from the back seat. 'Here we are,' he said, 'there's a pub.'

Indeed there was. Cigarette smoke was pouring from the windows, voices could be clearly heard in raucous celebration as we got out of the car. I was about to hang back, but Jack strenuously urged me across the road.

The door was solidly and massively locked. 'Hell,' said Jack.

'That's closed Father,' said a loud voice from across the street. 'Won't be open till later.'

The voice belonged to a tall policeman swaying gently on the balls of his feet. The law. We had a pronouncement from the law. Even though the pub was obviously bursting at the seams and doing a roaring trade, it was closed. The law said so. Jack led us a mere twenty yards down the road to the village's other alcoholic establishment. No policeman stood outside it, and the earlier guardian of the law obviously had tunnel vision. The door was welcomingly open and everybody was satisfied.

One of Jack's other sons, deprived by his position in the order of children, of any hope of inheriting the farm had abandoned the land, married and taken a pub in Galway. We were there several times during the course of the holiday, always received with the most exhausting kindness. But Liam too (that was his name) had the same peculiar attitude to law, that if you pretended it wasn't there, it would go away.

His pub was in a five-storey tenement-type building in the main square of Galway, One night we were returning from some jaunt long after midnight when Michael again, always ready, said, 'Let's have a last quick one at Liam's.'

'For Heaven's sake,' I remonstrated, 'the poor lad will be long in his bed at this time.'

'Liam in bed?' gurgled Michael. 'It's barely breakfast time for him!'

Sure enough as we pulled up outside, lights were on, the noise was enormous. Liam was doing good business. But just as surely the door was locked. I sighed. But Michael beat on the door and roared to his brother to open up. There was a long pause, and then way up above us on the top floor of the building a sash window was raised and a pyjama-clad figure peered out.

'What are you doing?' said Liam, 'waking decent people at this time of night.'

'For God's sake Liam,' said Michael, 'it's myself and Father Dermot. Open up.'

'Yerra why didn't you say so instead of making me dash all the way up here and put on my pyjamas. I thought it was the police.'

How Liam could have imaged that the police, if they had been there, would ever have been deceived by his pyjamas, when all the evidence of sight and sound testified that drinking on a large and noisy scale was going on down below, I never could fathom. But the police it seemed shared the same healthy disrespect for evidence. The door was closed, therefore there was no drinking. As a policeman in Galway it wouldn't do to have any other attitude.

And so the days went by. It was a change and a rest and a contrast to the grim dirt of Brimley. But more than that, those days reminded me that whether in Galway or Brimley people were people, their qualities and failings binding them so much more closely than geography or nationality might seem to separate them. I left my gentle wild anarchic hard-working cousins in the west and returned. I was happy to have seen them, and happy to be returning to my other people in Brimley.

## CHAPTER TWELVE

I STEPPED from the train in Brimley almost a year to the day since my first dramatic appearance. No trips, no panic, no homburg this time. But there was one happy similarity between the two arrivals. Amos was there to meet me.

'Hallo Amos. This is very kind of you. How on earth did you know when I'd be arriving?'

'Well,' said Amos with pontifical precision. 'I knew you were due back today. There are only three trains. I knew you wouldn't be on t'morning one, so I just came to meet the other two. Did you have a good holiday?'

'Yes I did Amos. But I'm glad to be back also. And here you are. Amos, I can't get over this, that you'd come to meet trains just on the off-chance that I'd be on them.'

As nearly as was possible to anyone of Amos's ruddy complexion, he blushed. 'Aw come on Father. You've been very good to me. It's the least I could do.'

'Very good to you Amos!' I was blushing now. 'It's exactly the reverse. I could not have coped with my first year in the parish without you. Let's get things straight.'

'Now don't let's stand here arguing. Get into t'car Father. Father Morrison will be glad to see you back. He's not been keeping well at all. I don't know if he'll be even fit for his own holiday.'

This was bad news and it sounded even more ominous as Amos revealed the details. A collapse during Sunday Mass, when Amos himself had to carry his frail figure off the altar. Three days in hospital in Barnsley while tests were done, though Amos did not know the outcome of these.

'He looks like a ghost,' said Amos. 'He won't admit he is ill, or even that he has been ill. You'll have to force him to be sensible Father.'

'Yes, yes I will Amos.' My voice I'm sure reflected the insecurity of that statement. I had never been able to to 'force' Father Morrison to do anything.

'I'm even more glad that I'm back. You'll have to help me, you know.' We formed our pact, vague and insubstantial though it was. And Sadie's greetings, after the first almost incidental enquiries about the holiday, reinforced the anxiety already firmly entrenched by Amos's concern.

'Father, it's almost as though he's just been willing himself to hold on until you got back. He knows everything will be in good hands now, so perhaps he'll relax and we can get him better.'

I was shocked at my first sight of him. The flesh seemed to have shrunk away from his large frame leaving him a walking skeleton with hollow eyes. His suit hung wretchedly from his wasted body. But the smile and the welcome were as warm as ever. Even Jasper joined the party leaping up, his front paws on my chest.

'Sit down Father and get yourself a drink. You too, Amos,' for Amos had accompanied me in. 'I've got something to tell you and it concerns you both.'

I poured two whiskys, my first since the Broadbents'. Father Morrison shook his head gently when I offered him one.

'I've been ill Father, while you've been away, as I'm sure Amos has told you. As I'm sure you can see,' pointing deprecatingly to his emaciated body. 'They took tests last week in Barnsley and they know now what it is. It's cancer Father, and you know what that means.'

Neither Amos nor I were capable of movement or speech.

'It's almost certain that I'll be dead in six months. Tom Murphy told me. I made him tell me. Can't have a priest, above everybody, moving into the last furlong of life without knowing it. So I'm quite resigned to it. I'll even welcome it in some ways, after the pain of the past few years.' There was a brief opening of the door into his mind and heart. Never before to anyone had he admitted pain or illness.

'However, they always think there's a chance. So they're taking me into hospital in Sheffield next week and they're going to operate. I don't think there's any hope but they do, or they say they do. I've been in touch with the Bishop to tell him. He had to know of course. He asked me did I want a temporary replacement while I was in hospital. It may be six weeks or more. I told him that you were more than capable of running things, so long as we had someone to help you with the Masses on Sunday. So he's leaving you in charge. I didn't tell him of course that we really have another curate. Amos. The first married curate ever, eh Amos?' That was the second time in a day that I had seen Amos blush.

'The other thing,' he continued, 'is that I would prefer the parishioners not to know. I don't know why, perhaps just an innate sense of privacy and a wish not to have a fuss made. So by all means put me on the list for prayers at Mass and in the evening services, but no hysteria, as though we're asking for a miracle or anything like that. And good luck Father in your first parish.' His eyes twinkled and he patted me on the shoulder. I found speech quite inappropriate. Can you wish good luck to a man who is expecting to die and painfully at that. I walked slowly from the room. Amos followed me as if by instinct up to my bed-sitter.

'You're going to have to help me Amos. I'll never manage on my own. The visiting and that side I'll cope with, but the money and administration is beyond me.'

'Now don't worry Father. It's all very straightforward. Sadie knows all the details of the housekeeping, bills and so on, so she'll keep you right about that side, just doing what Father normally does. And I'll be around most of t'time, because I'm preparing for t'Parish concert. It's all arranged with Father Morrison, and I'm sure he'd want it to go on. If we cancelled it now it would be a right give-away that there was something seriously wrong with him. And he doesn't want that does he? So I'll keep popping in in case there's anything you need advice about. Not that I'm in a real position to give advice, but I suppose it always helps to talk to someone about problems.'

So it was arranged. On the Tuesday Tom Murphy came around and collected Father Morrison to take him to Sheffield. 'I'll be going down fairly often,' he said to me, 'so any time you want to go just give me a ring. Not for the first week or so. It's a major operation and however it goes, he's not going to be feeling like visitors for at least a week. Give me a ring eh?'

Father Morrison left with the same courage and cheerfulness that he had always shown. He was more concerned that I wouldn't be overburdened, than about his own more terrible problems. I settled down in the house which was suddenly frighteningly empty.

The word got around of course as word always does, and short of telling absolute lies I had to acknowledge that Father was seriously ill. Sympathy and encouragement was universal. Father Morrison had been with his people for many years, and miners are intensely loyal. He was well loved. There was at least one odd side-effect.

Kathleen O'Malley was a strapping, healthy-looking wife. Her discovery that she was pregnant for the first time after several years of 'trying' (the mind boggled!) was greeted with delight by herself, her husband, a miner also, her parents, and if she could bring it about, by everyone in the town. It struck therefore as almost a national disaster when shortly after the pregnancy was confirmed, she was afflicted with German measles. Everybody, except me, knew that German measles contracted by a mother-to-be in the early weeks of pregnancy has up to a 50% chance of damaging the baby. How she had caught the disease nobody knew. There seemed to be no other cases in Brimley. Presumably a chance encounter.

Her doctor, Tom Murphy's partner and not himself a Catholic, strongly advised her to have a termination. The risk of giving birth to a blind or brain-damaged child was far too high to warrant the continuation of the pregnancy. He even asked me to persuade her. I was sufficiently unsure about the application of church law in this particular case to agree to see Kathleen, whatever about trying to persuade her.

The disease itself is so mild that by the time I got to Kathleen she was fully restored to the ruddiest of health. The small miner's cottage seemed to have its work cut out to contain her phsyical exuberance. She was not showing the pregnancy yet, but her whole being radiated content and fulfilment. And she was a very big girl.

'Well then Kathleen, you seem absolutely recovered. How are you feeling now?'

'Oh wonderful Father. It was nothing at all. Just a little rash for a couple of days. I'd been feeling a bit sick in the mornings with the baby but it seems to have cleared up even that. That's one miracle for you.' I wasn't sure I liked the sound of that, and how right I was.

'That doctor,' she said, her face reddening with outrage, 'that Halliday one, you know Father, he wants me to get rid of the baby. Tells me it's pretty certain to be deformed or something by the measles. Now let me tell you Father, as I've already told him, there's no chance of that. God hasn't been so good to me after all this time to let me conceive, and then to have the baby born blind or whatever. and if it takes a miracle to bring a healthy baby into the world, then a miracle I'm having. We're praying for a miracle for Father Morrison aren't we? We'll get that and we'll get mine too.'

I sat stunned. In face of that incredible faith, how could I possibly quote the medical statistics, and even less the observable percentage of cases where God did indeed allow children, expected with equal fervour and delight, to be born deformed, deficient and even dead? I dare not point out that if she backed her miracle double of Father Morrison and her baby, any bookie would be delighted to give her odds of a thousand to one. Before I could open my mouth she continued.

'Just to be on the safe side, I'm starting a Novena to Our Lady of Good Hope. I won't have it finished by the time Father Morrison is better, but that at least will be proof that my baby will be alright too. So stop looking so flabbergasted Father. Look on the bright side. Everything is going to be fine.'

Brimley, the land of miracles? It seemed a hard idea to swallow. But over the weeks Kathleen gathered together crowds of well-wishers and believers in miracles. Attendance at the Novena services on a Wednesday night broke all records. Where before we had three or four dozen pious souls, now there were literally hundreds. I absolutely refused to announce that the prayers were being said for Father Morrison's miraculous recovery, coupled with (as the toastmasters say) the safe delivery of a healthy child to Kathleen.

But they knew that's what it was all about, and they knew that I knew. I had the air of a hunted rabbit, they had the sublime certainty that God was in their team. I had always been a bit of a sceptic about miracles. They seemed a quite unnecessary and rather theatrical addition to the solidity of our faith. As a result I spent a very uncomfortable series of weeks. Father Morrison's operation had been satisfactorily completed but neither the doctors nor he himself knew whether the danger had been caught in time. I carefully avoided telling him of the miracle-seekers, but I might have saved myself anxiety. Somebody leaked the secret to him. 'I don't think they'll ever want me back in Brimley,' he said to me one night in mock sorrow. 'I hear you've taken over entirely, packed the church with devout parishioners. I could never do it.' He roared with a heartiness which in itself seemed to signify that his old self was being restored. I blushingly apologized for my silence. I hadn't wanted to worry him, I said.

'Worry me! I'm delighted. Whatever the reason, if you pack that old crowd of sinners into the church regularly, it can only do them good. It might even do me good!' The twinkle in his eye indicated that he, as much as I, rather doubted that. And then Nellie Ryan happened.

Nellie was like Father Morrison. For years she had been suffering the pains of the damned in her stomach without ever telling anyone. Only in the last few weeks, it appeared, had she told Tom Murphy. He came to me one day, sad in the face.

'I've bad news about Nellie, Father. Nellie Ryan, you know. She came to me only recently with terrible pains in the stomach. Had 'em for ages apparently. I whipped her into hospital, they did the tests, and she's riddled with cancer. No chance even of operating. Poor soul if she'd came months or perhaps even years ago, we might have been able to catch it. But now! They've sent her home Father. She asked to be told, so I told her. Some you do, some you don't, but Nellie's a fine woman and there'd be no point in lying to her.'

'I'll go round straight away Tom. This is terrible. First Father Morrison and now Nellie. And that mad woman

Kathleen O'Malley making such a production of it. She'll add poor Nellie to the list when she hears. Three miracles she'll want now.'

'Oh she's done that already Father. Nellie was always at church anyway, so everybody knows. It's getting a bit like Lourdes!' My heart sank. But Nellie had to be seen whether or not she was on the miracle-roster. Nellie's piety was strong and firm-rooted. Would not I thought be too much in sympathy with miracle melodrama. I took my way sadly to her house.

In the house when I arrived were Nellie, Tom Murphy and Matt McGinley. Matt had apparently caught Tom just as he was leaving the presbytery and taken him swiftly to Nellie's. She had had the most terrible bout of sickness, vomited in a way that Tom in all his experience had never seen before. She was lying now exhausted but cheerful on the couch in her spotless little room. Matt had cleared up the mess.

'I'm a silly woman Father. I'm sorry to have dragged you out. I feel so much better now anyway.'

'Come on now Nellie,' said Tom, 'I'll take you into hospital. They'll look after you at least for a while.'

'Hospital nothing. If I'm going to die I'll die in me own bed. This big lug here will look after me, won't you Matt?' Matt nodded silently, tears welling from his eyes. And despite all the kindly protests and logic of Tom and myself, that's how it was left. Nellie wouldn't budge.

'I'll come round every day to see her,' said Tom to me as we moved out of the little close. 'When she gets a lot worse I'll have to ignore her protests. Good and all as he is, poor Matt just couldn't do all that was needed for a dying woman.'

That was a Tuesday. The following night, Novena night, in the middle of the miracle-hunters sat Nellie, and by her side an abashed-looking Matt, who had obviously been dragooned into escorting her. There was one miracle anyway, getting Matt back into a church after all these years. I think that I was more embarrassed than he was.

A couple of weeks later Tom came into the presbytery again a frown of sheer bewilderment on his face.

'I just don't believe this,' he said. 'It's too early to be sure anyway but all the signs are there. Father Morrison is actually putting on weight (which I'd noticed) which would be impossible if the cancer were still there. And all the signs of terminal disease are fading rapidly. It very much looks, against all the odds, as though the surgery may have nipped it in the bud.'

I grinned with delight and did a dervish dance of glee around the room.

'Have you told Sadie? She'll be over the moon.'

'Hang on Father. That's only the half of it, much as I know you'd be so delighted about Father Morrison. Nellie Ryan. I took her back to the hospital for more tests and they say that her cancer too seems to have become inoperative. Whether she vomited it all up that time, which is almost medically impossible, or what, I don't know. And guess what's happening?'

'Oh no. Don't tell me. Kathleen O'Malley is claiming them both as miracles. Oh my God, what can we do?'

'What can we do? You just get into that pulpit on Wednesday and tell them straight. First that we don't know at all whether either Father Morrison or Nellie is going to pull through. And second, even if they do, there's no connection between this miracle-movement and what's happened. If they do pull through, it'll be for purely natural causes, even if we don't know what they are. You've got to do it Father, otherwise an awful lot of people are going to get awfully hurt, thinking that miracles of healing are available on tap, like a Heavenly National Health. It's just pure coincidence. It's a terrible thing to say, but I could almost wish that Kathleen's baby would be born with some injury. But the baby won't be born for four months yet, and it always had a fifty-fifty chance of being perfectly normal.'

I took Tom down to Father Morrison's study and we savaged a bottle of whisky. The occasion demanded it. But even under the glow of the alcohol, the picture refused to brighten. We gloomily bade each other goodnight. I awaited Wednesday with dread.

On the Tuesday however, Father Morrison was released from hospital. Although he was still weak, and under orders to convalesce in the house, and then take his delayed holiday, he insisted on going into the pulpit on the Wednesday. It was his job he said to stop the miracle-mongering before it got out of hand. Despite my worries about his health, I was relieved to let him do so.

'My dear people,' he said, 'I owe you all such a debt of thanks for your prayers over these weeks. None of us know yet whether I'm really better, or just showing a temporary improvement which is common in these cases. But I do know that your prayers have given me great strength and consolation to face whatever the Lord wishes for me, be it life or death. There's no miracle, my dear people, except the human miracle of your kindness and faith. That would be there whether I'd died in hospital or not. That's what we should be thankful for. God knows far better than we do what's best for us, and all the praying in the world isn't going to change His mind on that. What you lovely people have done is to put yourselves and your wishes into His hands, to tell Him that you trust Him completely. And that's a miracle, as so few of us do so trust Him. We always think we know better than He does. So keep up your praying, for me, for Mrs Ryan, for Mrs O'Malley, for yourselves, always remembering what you are really doing. You are putting your faith in Him, in what He knows to be best, and your prayers are always answered, even if most of the time, not in the way that *you* think they ought to be. God bless you, my children, and thank you.'

He was clearly exhausted as he came down from the pulpit. There wasn't a dry eye in the place. I compared his approach to the ghastly bungling that I would have made of it, and blessed him and his wise humanity. But you can never get the better of a woman, even in church. I met Kathleen after the service.

'I don't care what he says, my baby's going to be a grand healthy baby. I *know* that's what God wants, so I'm going to keep coming to the Novena.'

'So am I,' said Matt McGinley. 'Anyone who loves Nellie as God obviously does, gets my vote.'

That really is a miracle, I thought.

# CHAPTER THIRTEEN

OVERSHADOWED by the miraculous events, and indeed made to seem trivial and pointless by them, preparations for the parish concert had nonetheless struggled along. The purpose of the concert was to raise funds for the Old Folks' treat at Christmas. When the first news of the seriousness of Father Morrison's illness had leaked out, various members of the concert party had suggested to Amos that the whole venture be scrapped. But between us we decided that whatever happened, the old people would still need and deserve their Christmas celebration, and that the concert should proceed. We did agree however to postpone the date until we knew more certainly of Father Morrison's condition. Now with the good news of his return, a fresh sense of urgency went into the preparations.

At first I was astounded that Amos should be both the producer and the M.C. His qualities were many, but I thought that his natural shyness and reticence would inhibit any chance of his coming over on a stage. Not a bit of it. The smell of the greasepaint or whatever, galvanized him, and he became a new person, a cross between Harry Secombe and Arthur Lowe. He had a deep and true bass voice which belted out a song as professionally as any concert artist. And his patter in introducing acts was hilarious and very well delivered. The choice of Amos then was obvious.

His main problem was to choose his fellow artists. There was no lack, rather the reverse, as hordes of parishioners offered their services. How to persuade most of them to step down without hurting their feelings, was the question. But here too Amos showed himself a master. Where I would weakly have surrendered to every claim, and had a cast of thousands, Amos was very discriminating. Or so he told me. When he finally assembled his group and presented their routines in rehearsal to me, I blenched to think of what he must have rejected, if these were the pick.

'Very . . . er . . . good Amos. They're . . . er . . . splendid. It'll be a marvellous concert.'

'Who are you kidding, Father? Most of them are absolutely dreadful. But it doesn't matter you know. The audience won't be coming to compare it with a Palladium show. They want to see our Sadie, or our Willie or their Uncle Fred. And what they do is of no great moment. So you can take that look of horror off you face, Father. It'll be a good family party and a great success and you'll get up at the end and say so, but don't let's kid ourselves that we're going to break into show business.'

Amos was, as always, correct, and I felt suitably rebuked. He printed posters, which were plastered all over the town, and began to sell tickets. Long before the two nights on which the concert was to run, every ticket was sold. Had we had room in the parish hall, we could have sold many more. So the end-product, funds for the old people was now amply assured.

Father Morrison had by this time progressed from convalescence to holiday, so that it was, as Amos had predicted, up to me to be the guest of honour, and thank both participants and audience for their work and co-operation. Despite my now long practice in the pulpit, and the beginnings of ease in that work, I did not look forward to these final speeches. I carefully prepared what I would say, even down to a couple of silly jokes, lest I be left tongued-tied. But on the night I was still uneasy.

The first night was as successful as Amos had promised: wild applause from the audience for every act, total attention to every word. Tom Murphy, surprisingly, was the final act, displaying a sweet Irish tenor voice in a selection of well-known songs. Even my little speech of thanks was rapturously received, and I came out of the hall with my ears glowing with pleasure.

But the second night was a very different story. It was raining for a start and our hall had long been in need of repairs, so that the audience already wet when they arrived, found streams of water pouring on them in various parts of the hall. That would have been tolerable, as they are a hardy lot in Brimley, but one of the most devastating streams fell directly on our pianist, Miss Grimswood. A fine musician and a willing helper in endeavours which must have crucified her musical sensibilities, she was not willing to sit under a fountain. So the piano had to be moved, and when she assumed her new position, she found she could no longer see the performer whom she would have to accompany. There followed then hideous grimaces directed round a corner to try to inform her that the singer or dancer was ready, and even worse, her usual adaptability to whatever mistakes, hesitations or repetitions the soloists might make, was totally impossible. It was like playing blind-man's buff with real blind people. The pleasure in watching our Annie was palpably lessened by the fact that Annie's screeches were very obviously out of tune with Miss Grimswood's playing. The audience began to be restive.

Even Amos's composure seemed to desert him. He got mixed up in his announcements, so that when he invited us to give a big hand for Tommy Thorburn who imagined himself to be a comedian, onto the stage trooped Sister Clare's dancing class. They stood in some embarrassment waiting for their introductory music from Miss Grimswood, while she sat back waiting for the embarrassing attempts at humour that passed for Tommy Thorburn's act. She couldn't see of course who was on the stage.

Willie, 'adultery' Willie, who by some monstrous casting error was one of the males in Sister Clare's troop, took it upon himself to rectify the error. Bursting from the group to the front of the stage he leaned outwards and roared to the invisible Miss Grimswood, 'It's us Sister. The dancers you know. It's not Mr Thorburn after all.' His heroic efforts won instant applause, and it was quick thinking. He smiled hugely and bowed to his audience and promptly overbalanced and fell off the stage. Even more hysterical applause greeted this spontaneous gesture, which was no consolation to Willie who had injured his person in several sensitive spots.

'Bloody and damn,' he shouted in pain and anguish and hobbled off into the wings. For some little time the concert proceeded according to plan and then on trotted Frank Nellis. Frank was a miner, and of the old school, and his legs were bent, partly from juvenile rickets, partly from the employment he had followed for over fifty years. One could kick a full-sized football straight through his legs while his feet were tight together. Not that this deformity in any way worried Frank. He had lived far too long and far too hard for him to have any time for sensitivity about his appearance. In a high-pitched voice he announced his programme, greeted with load cheering. Frank was a popular artist. He played the spoons. Yes, spoons. With almost miraculous dexterity he could beat out a rhythm out of two ordinary spoons that would have been no disgrace for Gene Krupa. Miss Grimswood never had any problems with Frank. He had a meticulous sense of timing.

The success of his act was restoring good humour to the audience. They clapped their hands and stamped their feet to his incredible rhythms. His pièce de résistance was part of the Overture to William Tell, where the music rises to an impossibly fast crescendo. After the final rattle of his spoons, Frank used to raise them high and smash them on to his leg as his conclusion. This night whether in excitement or miscalculation, he brought them down in a fearful wallop straight on to his knee. Fairly obviously he knocked his kneecap clean out. His leg collapsed, he collapsed. At first the audience thought this was part of the act and roared their approval, until above the applause could be heard the shrill shrieking of Frank. Not just shrieking but a stream of miners' oaths which would have taken the paint off the door. He was clearly in great pain, but mothers who were more concerned that their children should not hear his obscene ravings, began to rise from their seats.

Onto the stage leapt Amos, himself looking rather like a Demon King. He scooped little Frank up in one brawny arm and scuttled off the stage with him. The audience subsided again and waited with exemplary patience until Amos reappeared, presumably having handed over the wailing Frank to the ministrations of Tom Murphy, who would be backstage, waiting his turn to perform. Amos restored good humour with a few deft witticisms, and raised the tone again with a spirited rendition of Old Man River. The evening was rescued.

After a couple of fairly harmless acts Lizzie Clark was introduced. Lizzie was enormous, but whereas weight and girth were almost necessities to most great sopranos, they simply existed on Lizzie. She was not a good soprano. With ear-splitting ferocity she sang every note stridently off-key. However, as Amos had said, we were not there to witness artistic excellence but to applaud honest and willing endeavour. There was plenty of that from Lizzie. Her final song was 'Danny Boy', a daunting melody with very wide range even for the trained singer. Lizzie murdered it at full blast. As she almost physically rose to its last high note, missing it with her usual precision and volume, there was a movement under her dress, and her long orange bloomers descended around her ankles. The elastic had obviously given up the ghost under the strain of that final mighty bellow. As I tried to avert my eyes the audience collapsed in mass hysteria, scarcely noticing Lizzie's frantic endeavours to pull up her drawers. She finally hobbled off to a wave of applause greater than any ever heard in Brimley.

How could anyone follow that? It was left for poor Tom Murphy, the last act of all, to try to round the concert off more sedately. A fulsome introduction by Amos served to reduce the hysterical laughter to some degree, and a stirring series of chords by Miss Grimswood brought them finally to order. Tom appeared. A brief moment of silence was followed by a redoubling of the laughter. Tom was in full evening dress, but his bow tie was anchored rather nonchalantly not between the points of his collar, but under his left ear. His legs appeared to be made of indiarubber as he moved slinkily towards the front of the stage.

'Ish got some shongs, shongs, to shing.'

Wild applause. What a wonderful imitation of a drunk. Only I, and I'm sure Amos, knew that it was no imitation. Tom was stewed to the gills. Sweat ran down me, as to the accompaniment of hysterical guffaws he went through his routine. No Irish bar had ever been treated to a more drunken exhibition. The people loved it and screamed for more. And Tom was only too happy to oblige. Swaying dangerously, grinning idiotically, he gave encore after encore. Finally Amos, pretending to be drunk also, put a half-nelson on him which threatened to break his arm and forced him off the stage. Even then he tried to come back, until Amos in mock rage chased him into the wings.

My speech of thanks was heartfelt. Thanks that it was over. I went backstage to view the casualties. Willie had an eye which was rapidly moving from purple to black. Frank lay panting on an old couch whimpering to himself as he waited for the ambulance that Sister Clare had sensibly called. Poor Lizzie was inconsolable. And Tom was snoring gently as he sat on the floor hugging his knees. It had all been a wonderful success.

As the audience filed out into the cool of the night, with the rain completely gone, there suddenly rang over the dark wet streets the strident demands of a siren. A short burst, a long burst, a short burst again. The effect was eerie.

'What on earth is that for?' I asked Amos.

'That, Father, means there's been an accident at the pit. A serious one, or they wouldn't ring that. We'd better get down there.'

## CHAPTER FOURTEEN

ALTHOUGH I had now been over a year in Brimley, lived among and come to know its dominant population, the miners, no thought of the terrible demands of their work, let alone the terrible dangers, had really crossed my mind. Miners just didn't talk about such possibilities. I had no idea, then, whether there had been disasters in this mine, or if so, when they had occurred. I cursed myself yet again for my blindness, my inability to see or think about anything that wasn't rammed down my throat. It was then with a humbling sense of apology that I turned to Amos.

'Are there frequent incidents in the mine? Are there likely to be many people hurt?'

'Father, something or other happens every week. But when they sound that siren you can be sure that it's no small accident involving just one or two, as it normally is. This is something big. Don't worry though, we've got teams ready, who'll know exactly what to do, if anything can be done. So grab your Holy Oils, Father and I'll rush you down there. I have to go, I'm the leader of one of the rescue teams.'

I rushed from the hall into the house, picked up my Holy Oils and my stole, told Sadie what was happening and where I would be.

'I'll get you a meal whenever you come in Father. On you go and God go with you.' Sadie obviously knew that there can be no predicted timetable for a mine accident. She probably had previous experience after all these years here with Father Morrison. Why had it never occurred to me to ask her? I rushed almost angrily into the night.

The whole of Brimley it seemed had gathered round the moon-like landscape which surrounded the pit. They were quiet, expectant, with no slightest sign of that febrile excitement common to crowds who gape eagerly at the scene of accidents, morbidly trying to glimpse disaster. There was an almost fatalistic patience here. Most of those who waited were, of course, women. The men were either in the mine, or quietly preparing in their various fashions to give what assistance they could. Amos drove straight through to the offices and washrooms which clustered near the pit-head. Ominously, several ambulances and fire engines stood waiting.

Amos hopped from the car without a backward word and disappeared into the offices. I climbed more slowly from his rickety old car, and stood sheepishly by it. Within minutes Amos was back.

'There's been a fair sized fall, Father, near one of the faces, and the one lad who managed to get clear says he saw fire, before the gallery was cut off. So there's thirty men caught behind that wall of rock and maybe they're all dead by now. There's one team down there now, more or less seeing what can be done, and as soon as they report, then me and my lot will go down. There's nothing much you can do Father. They won't let you go down just now. Apart from the danger, you'd just be in the way. There's not all that much space to work in as it is.' He smiled and patted me comfortingly on the shoulder. 'If there's anything you can do Father then we'll come and get you. You'll just have to wait like all the rest of them. Miners' families are used to waiting, you know. They're always prepared for t'worst. Things really haven't changed much since those days you read about in history wi't'little trappers and t'rest. If summat goes wrong, there's still very little anybody can do. It's a hard life. Nobody really knows except t'miners. Perhaps you'll understand us a bit better after this.' He grinned shyly again. And at that moment the great wheel on top of the headstock began to turn. 'That's them coming up Father. I'd better go and be ready.' He moved off lightly on his little legs under the vast torso. I stood and waited. Another van drew up nearby out of which came three figures. The one I recognized was the Reverend Armstead, the Methodist minister. We had exchanged, 'Good days,' as we passed, but had never spoken. His two companions were ladies, who proceeded to the back of the van and began to lift out large containers. They seemed very heavy.

'Let me help you, please,' I said to one of the ladies.

'That's very good of you sir. If you could help with that soup over into the office, I'd be very grateful.'

I helped to lift the large billy-can into the building.

'Father Kennedy, isn't it?' said the minister. 'I'm Armstead. Thank you very much. An awful business and this is all we can do to help. It'll be hours yet you know before they even find out if anything can be done.' He spoke in the soft sing-song of the Welsh valleys.

'You'll have seen this before,' I said. 'It's my first experience and I feel a bit lost.'

'Oh yes, you will. But sadly you'll get used to it if you stay in Brimley long. If there's a lot killed, it'll rate a few words on the wireless in the news, and perhaps a few lines in the paper. But there'll never be a word about the smaller accidents. Only the miners and us know about them. Nobody really cares, you know, for all they're always talking about it.'

As he spoke I saw two groups of men, one moving from the pithead and the other moving towards it. They met, coalesced very briefly, and then separated again. I recognized the burly figure of Amos leading the way to the cage, and among those following him the tall figure of Matt McGinley. The rescuers were moving in, but there was to be no statement as to what the prospects of actual rescue were. Word gradually filtered out confirming what Amos had originally heard. The rain began to fall again steadily.

I had been embarrassed at the obvious readiness of the Methodists to provide practical help for the squads of men who in relays would risk their lives to try to save their fellows. Father Morrison would have known what to do. Here was I standing helplessly, doing nothing. I need not have worried. Within minutes two more vans drew up, both equipped in much the same way as that of Reverend Armstead. One held Mr Baraclough, the Church of England vicar, and his helpers; the other, three of my ladies from the Mothers' Union. Or two of my ladies and Maeve. They knew what to do and didn't need me to organize them. I blushed again at my own incompetence as I gratefully helped them with their containers.

'Tom's on his way Father,' said Maeve, smiling her understanding smile. 'It's taken quite a lot of coffee to sober him up, and I had to get that monkey-suit off him. But there's rarely any hurry in these things Father, so it'll be alright. Poor Father, you look blue with the cold. Come in and have a cup of soup.'

'No, no thanks, Maeve. I'm fine. It's the men who'll need that. I just feel so useless. Everybody else knows what to do, and does it so well and without any fuss. Even the wives mothers, children, just wait. They know that everything that can be done is being done.'

I looked round at them. It was past midnight. The big lights of the mine buildings shone through the rain onto the largely silent and immobile crowd huddling together as if to keep off the wet. No one thought of leaving. Their places were with their men, whether those trapped in a possible inferno, or those working furiously to get to them.

'Now don't be silly Father. Just you come in here. There's no good you can be doing standing outside.'

Gently but firmly she led me in. Even Maeve, with no husband or son in that hell below the ground, saw her place as here, with the community. My other two ladies were moving over to the waiting women, to bring them a hot cup of something, to ease the long desperations of the night.

About three o'clock, Amos and his band of rescuers came to the surface, as another group relieved them. He and all of them were black and sweat stained. They made no move to wipe off the dirt as they gratefully poured mugs of hot soup into their parched throats. They would be going back down.

'We're not half-way there yet, Father,' said Amos. 'It'll be well after daylight before we get to any of 'em, if they're still alive. We've heard nothing, and they normally tap out some kind of message. And it's as hot as hell, so God knows what we're going to find when we do get through. Why don't you take my car and get a few hours' sleep and come down again in the morning after Mass. There's nowt you can do here till then.'

'I'll take the car Amos, thank you, just to let Sadie know what's happening. I'm sure the poor woman will be up like everybody else. But I'm not going to bed. It would be like betraying all these people, as if I didn't care. I'll be back in half an hour and I'll go back up at seven and say the Mass. Maybe by that time if there's anything for me to do . . .' I tailed off. Amos clapped me again on the shoulder with his dirt-stained hand. It was, for me, an act of approval, a recognition that in some indefinable way I was at last really a part of this community. I felt a warm glow rising through me.

'I'll see you soon Amos.'

'Aye lad.'

Sadie was nodding in her chair. No thought of bed for her either. She had to stay in the house in case of any calls, but she too was sharing the night vigil. These were her people. She came fully awake as I came in, listened with attention as I made the situation at the mine clear to her.

'We can only pray Father. Sit down and I'll make you a quick sandwich and a cup of tea. You'll be wanting to get back down there. And after Mass you can have a proper breakfast before you go back again. It'll be then that your work will begin, if there are any of the poor men left alive.'

The night crawled on leaden feet. I left the little huddle of helpers and the minister and the vicar about half past six, said the Mass for the small number of people who braved every morning, and returned to the mine. Amos's group were just readying themselves for their next shift.

'We'll get through this time Father. Doc Murphy's coming down with us, and I'd stand by if I were you in case anyone needs the Last Rites.'

The dawn had come up hazily and redly, promising that the rain which had lessened through the night would not be long in returning. Great black slicks of water covered the forecourt of the mine, but the womenfolk of Brimley remained silent and expectant. Not even the Last Trump would move them until they knew what had happened to their men. The great wheel spun again, lowering Amos and Tom and the rest below. This time with grim certainty three or four of the firemen who had been standing by in relays accompanied them, as did some of the ambulancemen with their stretchers. The long vigil was nearly at an end. But what would they find at the end of that fearsome gallery?

Less than an hour later, the wheel spun again and a call came for us the churchmen to go below. We had already been fitted up with clothing and helmets. My heart was thumping painfully as I moved to the cage. Never before had I thought to go down this great shaft. All my people worked down in those underground tunnels. Why had it never occurred to me to see for myself the conditions of life which were normal for them, without which sight I could never fully appreciate their lives and feelings? We came to a halt, and the gates were pulled back.

We were loaded aboard a kind of flat trailer with railings, used normally I presumed for transporting the miners to and from the coal face. I was astounded at the distance we travelled before pulling up. Ahead, behind a scurrying of men, I could see the great blockage sealing off the gallery from roof to floor. A small opening had been cut into it, no more than four feet high. Tom Murphy, blackened like a miner himself, was just crawling out of it.

"There's no point in your going through gentlemen, you'll only slow down the people being brought out. There are fifteen of them still alive, though most of them are badly burned. They managed to huddle under a ventilation shaft and get air. They need hospital treatment very quickly, so would you attend to them as they pass. We've found four dead, burned to death, so the other eleven must be buried under that.' He pointed to the grim mass behind him. 'There's no hope for them, but we'll get out the living and the four dead we've found first, before there's any attempt to dig them out. They've got the fire under control now, so the real danger's past, as far as danger is ever past in a mine.'

He sounded immensely weary, immensely depressed. The head of the first stretcher carried by Matt McGinley appeared through the narrow opening. With a speed which was remarkable for being totally controlled, all fifteen of the injured were brought through, loaded on the trailer and taken on their way to the shaft. Each of us, the three Reverends, sought out our own men, and ministered to them in our different ways as they passed us. My stomach turned at the horrific burns which disfigured them, at the mixture of pain, relief and hope which filled their staring eyes.

Following the sick came the even more grisly figures of the dead men. There had not been time or room to carry down the sheets or blankets to cover them, and they lay twisted and deformed nakedly on their stretchers. I raised my hand in a despairing blessing over them, thought of the sadness and emptiness of their families clustered round the pit-head, hope finally gone. Two of them were parishioners of ours, whose cosy and cheerful cottages I had often visited. What would happen now to their wives and children? I knew, even as I considered the question, what the answer would be. The whole living community would rally round, their own gratitude at being spared the Angel of Death this time, expressed in a caring and concern which could rise only in a mining town.

Amos was the last out of the narrow tunnel. 'There's no hurry for those poor lads under that. We're due up anyway. Come on then Father. You look as though you've looked the Lord of Death in the face yourself. I don't say you'll get used to it. I hope you never do. But it'll never be as bad for you as this time.'

The journey along the echoing gallery seemed even longer this time. The empty walls, the staring lights, the supporting props betokened a way of life which could always end in a holocaust at the end of the track. There was not a word said as we all were hoisted sadly to the surface. The rain was still holding off, but the stark outlines of the wheel and the buildings were darkly reflected in the black pools left from the night's downpour. The women had dispersed, certainty of hope or sadness now in their hearts in place of the fatalistic worry of the night.

I went to the houses of the two dead miners before I went back to the presbytery. In the first house there was numb acceptance.

'Thank you for everything Father. I know there was nothing more you or anyone could have done. And thanks for your offer of help. We'll get by somehow. Thanks Father.'

But at Gordon Burnett's house, the sadness and the sorrow were more open. Gordon had been one of our collectors in church whenever his shifts allowed him, his wife was prominent in the Mothers' Union, his two children of six and eight were among the happy delights in the school. They stood clinging to each other in a tragic grouping, their sobs and tears shaking their bodies.

'Why did it have to be Gordon, Father? We need him so much and he was so alive. He would have been off today and we were all going to go to t'moors. What are we going to do Father? What are these poor children going to do? Oh why Father, why?'

'There's no comfort I can give you my dear. It's God's will, and that's no real consolation.'

The two children released from their mother's embrace came over to me and folded themselves sadly into my arms. It was as though they sought in my poor body some substitute however weak and temporary for their dead dad. I wept harshly and unshamedly. If I could not share the joys of fatherhood, I could at least weep for the loss felt by these two little ones. I returned to the presbytery feeling old and frail.

'I've put a bottle in your bed Father. Come and sit here first and have this brandy I've poured for you.'

Dear Sadie put her arms round me as I sat and pressed my weeping eyes to her shoulder. She patted me and crooned over me as a mother with a child. I could say nothing. I drank the brandy and stumbled blindly to my bedroom.

The bodies of the other eleven men were brought out during the day. In the evening I received a visit from the vicar, Mr Barraclough.

'Mr Armstead and myself have been talking Father, and we'd like to have a common funeral for all the men. Would you feel able to join us Father? We'd appreciate it very much and I think the townspeople would like it. So often we appear to be pulling in different directions. It would be nice if we could show them at least this once that we're united in love, and in sharing their sorrow.'

I was so near to tears that I had to stand up and blow my nose very loudly. 'I should be very honoured to join you, Mr

Barraclough. If you please to organise things, because I'm so new to everything, I shall be very happy to fit in wherever you think best.'

The funeral was indeed a joining together of the whole town. We all held services in our respective churches and then, all walking, joined into one procession to the cemetery just on the edge of town. The sun shone palely on the scene, as if weeping with us all, and yet promising a light of hope to come. As the fifteen bodies were lowered into the communal grave, all of us, Methodist, Anglican, Catholic, and many, I'm sure of no allegiance at all, joined together to sing 'Oh God our help in ages past'.

'It's times like this that show what religion's all about,' said Amos as we walked back from the cemetery. 'In a way I think those poor lads achieved something in their death, that they could never have brought about in life. God's a rum 'un, isn't He, Father?'

# CHAPTER FIFTEEN

FATHER MORRISON, who had been extending his convalescence and taking his holiday at the same time, had not been able to get back to Brimley in time for the communal funeral. He had been staying with some friends of his in their villa in Taormina in Sicily, a gorgeous medieval town with Greek and Roman ancestry, clinging to the side of a mountain in sight of Mount Etna. But he did cut his visit short, so that he might be back among his people in their hour of tragedy. He still looked very frail, though he pooh-poohed any sympathy and declared himself as fit as a fiddle. Those of us who loved him were gladdened by his reappearance but fearful at the same time that any extra exertion would take too great a toll on his still emaciated body. He was still under strict orders from Tom to restrict his activities and above all not to spend too much time on his feet.

'If I can walk the hills of Taormina then I'm sure Brimley can hold no dangers for me.'

'And if you go on being so stubborn,' replied Tom, 'I shall have no option but to hospitalize you again for your own good. Come on now Father. They've pulled you back from the edge of the grave, don't be silly enough to jump in.'

Grudgingly he gave his assurances to both Tom and myself that he would take things very easily. Neither of us put too much faith in the promises, and we agreed to keep careful eyes on him. I insisted for a start that whatever visiting of parishioners had to be done would be done by me. 'It will mean that most of them won't see a priest quite so often Father, but I'm sure that won't do them any great harm. I'll see all the ones who need a visit, just as often of course, so nobody is going to be neglected. And I'll take particular care of those families affected by the mine disaster. Some of those men that survived, Father, are never going to be able to work again. I know we can't keep them, but we can, I'm sure, with your permission, allot as much of our charitable funds as possible to them.'

'Of course, of course Father. You're beginning to sound like a parish priest. I'll have to watch it or you'll be putting *me* out to grass! Seriously though, that's one thing I must do and you must allow me to do. I must go to see all those families. I owe it to them as their parish priest.'

'Well, only on condition that you let me borrow Amos's car and drive you around. That's at least fifteen families which is far too far to walk, and the interviews are likely to be very harrowing. They were for me.'

Father Morrison agreed. 'We will have to get a parish car. It's ridulous that poor Amos should have to keep lending us his and anyway I'm sure it's going to pack up one of these days.'

'It's like you Father,' I said. 'With care it'll go on for ever.'

'Away with you. Get the car and come back for me. I want to see those people as soon as possible.'

The round of the families was very tiring, the more so because the grief and real distress took so much out of us. Father Morrison insisted on seeing them all that one day, and thus it was well into evening before we came to the last family. By accident of geography it was again at the Burnett household that we finished. The children's sorrow was already muted. It would come in short terrible bursts, but their young spirits, by instinct of survival, shrugged it off much more quickly than did adults. Mrs Burnett seemed to have aged and withdrawn into herself.

'Very good of you to come Father,' she said to Father Morrison. 'I'm sure you're not well enough yourself to be traipsing round the lot of us. It would have waited. Nothing's going to bring Gordon back, now or later.' Her voice broke and the tears started to her eyes. A tall young woman with a positive mane of glorious russet hair, rose from where she was sitting on the other side of the fire. She put her arms round Mrs Burnett and soothed her racking sobs.

'I'm sorry, Father, Fathers,' she said eventually. 'I know it's silly but I just can't stop it.'

'Cry yourself out Margaret dear,' said Father Morrison, his own voice by no means under control. 'It does help, surprisingly. and if anyone has, you have all the reason in the world to cry. My poor poor lady.'

'I'm forgetting my manners too Father. This is my sister Jennifer. She's with the police in York, and she's taken her leave to come down and be with us. It's very good of her. I don't know what we'd do without her.'

'Hallo, Fathers,' said Jennifer. Her voice was deep and warm. A beautiful young woman was Jennifer.

'Now Margaret,' said Father Morrison, 'I know it's far too early for you even to be thinking about things like money, and I know most of it will be handled officially through the Coal Board, so that you don't need to worry. But when things have settled down, and you're able to see the future a bit more clearly, I want you to come to us and let us know if there's anything at all that you need. We'll be proud and happy to do whatever we can to help.'

We rose to go. The two children were wide-eyed with awe. *Two* priests in the house at once was something they'd never seen. Jennifer shook us by the hand, and her own hand was firm and strong.

'Goodbye then, and God bless and help you all,' said Father Morrison.

He went straight to his bed on return and willingly stayed there the whole of the next day. He had in a way, taken all the sadness of these good people onto his own shoulders, and they had crumpled and bowed him. Perhaps I was lucky or insensitive or both, but to my youth, as to the children's, death was still remote, however close it might approach, as it had done so tragically this last week. It may have been for that reason, that I noticed much more than usual how many old people there were in the parish. Not that the prospect of death seemed to inhibit their enjoyment of life, however near it might seem to be.

Winnie Smallwood, an aged and wrinkled crone of very uncertain temper, still kept her bottle of Guinness in a potty under her bed, as though in an ice-bucket. When I first went, she offered me a drink of Guinness, and since it was a hot day, and I was gaspingly thirsty, I had accepted her offer. Only then had I seen where she stored it, but drink it I must, though I gagged at every mouthful.

Joanie Telfer was another. I think she had always had 'a bit missing' as they used to say in Brimley. She was however quick enough to pick up Tom Murphy's suggestion that every time I asked her how she was, she was to say that she'd 'had it all out'. Tom knew well enough how embarrassed I would be by that intimate confession. Joanie knew also, as every time I went into the house, she would repeat, with a cackle and a most unsavoury leer, 'I've 'ad it all out you know, Father.' No fear of the living or dead with Joanie.

Pipes were Amy Lister's weakness. When I first started smoking, I offered Amy a cigarette one day.

'No thanks Father, I smoke a pipe.'

I roared with what I thought was the expected laughter, until looking onto her mantelpiece, there I saw a dozen or so white clay pipes.

'I've allus smoked 'em.' Her eighty years old eyes crinkled with laughter. I was sure Amy would go over the threshold of eternity still chomping happily on her clay pipe.

They refreshed me, those old people. There was no fear of death among them. They had been through all the joys and sorrows of life. Death when it came would be one more, if indeed the final, milestone to be passed. Even Jasper as he came round with me seemed to sense their serenity. He would hunker down in total content as I chatted with the old people, sure that he would not be fondled or messed about, as he was so often by children and younger adults. He was a dog for the quiet life was Jasper.

So as the days slipped by, and as Father Morrison slowly began to regain some semblance of his strength, the autumn days drew on. It was one of those crisp lovely times with the touch of early morning frost and the halo round the moon at night. I savoured the sharp freshness of it as I walked back into the presbytery one night. A police car was parked outside the door and all the lights in the house seemed to be on.

'Thank goodness you're back Father,' said Sadie. 'I had all on to stop Father Morrison going out himself.'

'What on earth has happened Sadie? Surely not another accident at the mine? I would have heard the siren, I'm sure.'

'No no Father. It's a young boy gone missing. The Lercaro boy, Daniel, I think his name is. Do you know him Father?'

'Yes I do Sadie. I'd better go through and see what's happening.' I knocked at Father Morrison's door. Inside an air of crisis pervaded the room. Father Morrison himself had his hair standing in an untidy aureole round his head, and a feverish light was in his eyes. Sitting hunched on his settee were Mr and Mrs Lercaro. I had never spoken to them, but I recognised them from those earlier days when we had the little trouble with Daniel. He was heavy and strong-boned, while her delicacy seemed only to emphasize an inner strength. I could see the likeness of Daniel in both of them. And they hated each other, I remember Father Morrison saying. The tableau was completed by two policemen whom I did not recognize. They were certainly not our local bobbies.

'Hallo Father, come in,' said Father Morrison, an air of something between relief and despair in his voice. 'We've got a problem here, did Sadie tell you? This is Mr and Mrs Lercaro and these gentlemen, Constables Rutter and Mason, is it, are from West Riding headquarters in Wakefield. Young Daniel has gone missing. He went out for a walk just after tea, as he often did, and just hasn't reappeared. I know it's not very late, but everywhere he might possibly be, he's not. It may be some kind of accident, or it may be even worse, a kidnapping. Mr and Mrs Lercaro won't mind if I say they are very well off, and such people can be targets for these kidnappers. The local police asked for help from Wakefield, and these good gentlemen are here to help direct the search. The police, Amos and others are out now rounding up people who are willing to help. They'll be at the Hall any time now. Fortunately it's a lovely clear night. I'm sure you'll want to help. Mr and Mrs Lercaro tell me Daniel is always talking about you and seems to like you a lot. So it would be a comfort to them if you would go. I wanted to go myself but . . . you know . . .'

'Thank you so much Father,' said Mrs Lercaro in a soft, tight voice. 'Daniel thinks the world of you.'

'I'll be happy to go, Mrs Lercaro, though why Daniel should think that way of me, I really don't know.'

'Good, Father.' A deep gruff voice came from Mr Lercaro. 'We'd better get back to the house in case there are any calls from . . . er . . . from anyone. Thank you all very much for your concern.' He shouldered his way to his feet, a big heavy man. He stretched his hand to help his wife. Fairly noticeably she ignored it. She moved with the grace of a ballet dancer. There was something unreal about them. Their child, the dark-eyed mysterious cherub, had disappeared. The most obvious reason was that in a desperate unhappiness, he had just run away. Without thought, without plan. To get away from that gnawing atmosphere of hate. And no one would put voice to this probability. We sat discussing accidents or kidnapping, while somewhere a young boy sat alone and afraid, with no one at all in the world to turn to. At least the young Burnetts still had their mother, their aunt, their schoolfellows. But Daniel, wherever he was, was alone. I felt sick to my stomach.

'Now please Father, just you go to bed,' I said to Father Morrison. 'Even if you don't sleep, you'll be resting. And there's nothing you can do. These good gentlemen and all the volunteers will search as best we can, and we'll give you reports as often as we can. Please Father, there's no point in your getting ill again.'

'He's right you know sir,' said one of the policemen. 'Frankly, I think our chances at night are pretty thin anyway, unless he's somewhere very obvious. We'll start over the hills from his home, but if he's fallen and is unconscious, even two hundred of us could miss him. I hope we don't, because these cold nights . . ' He said no more.

There were fifty of us, a remarkable number given that every one had a job to go to in the morning, had been working all day. Given too, that the Lercaros were hardly known to this crowd which was made up predominantly of miners. They were toffs and never mixed with the locals. Tom Murphy appeared as we were about to set out. He went to the sergeant.

'I can't come with you Alan. I'm on call tonight and Doctor Halliday is away. But don't hesitate to call me if there's anything I can do. I can roust up the hospitals better than anybody if there's any need. Good luck to you all.'

He waved and was off. We were divided into four groups, each under the command of one of the policemen. Our local sergeant was in overall control as he obviously knew the ground better than the Wakefield men. I found myself in a group which included Miss Jennifer, the aunt of the Burnett children. She was very self-possessed.

'It's the least I could do to repay the kindness of all the people I've met here,' she said to me as we moved off side by side. 'Anyway I am in the police, so perhaps my training may come in useful.'

'I can't imagine you in the police. You seem far too . . . er . . . I don't know how to put it.' And in a rush. 'You're far too beautiful to be in the police.' It was well that it was night as I felt myself blushing furiously.

'Thank you very much kind sir.' Her peal of laughter rang incongruously through the subdued searchers. 'Sorry, I shouldn't laugh, either at you or in these circumstances. You pay a nice compliment Father. Thank you. Incidentally I might say the same about you. You're far too good-looking to be a priest. What a waste.' She laughed again though more quietly and intimately.

I shied away in embarrassment from further conversation. In any case, the harsh business of searching the hills and hollows had begun in earnest. There were no landmarks, no obvious trails. It was a slogging grind of trying to cover every inch. By four in the morning it was pitch dark. The moon was down and little light survived. The sergeant wisely called a halt and led us all back to Brimley.

'There's just no point in going on. Thanks very much all of you. We'll try to get some more volunteers and start again at first light. Thanks very much again and good-night.'

'Goodnight Father,' said Jennifer to me as she moved off with the rest of them down towards their houses in Brimley. 'It was nice talking to you. I'll be back in the morning.

Perhaps we'll be in the same group again.' Her warm throaty chuckle floated away down the street.

'Goodnight Jennifer,' I called after her, feeling deliciously foolish. I watched the frosted breath around their heads fade and disappear.

Sadie, ever thoughtful, was waiting for me with hot soup. Even Jasper roused from his sleep, seemed glad to see me. We let him out to perform his nightly offices.

'Father fell asleep a couple of hours ago. It would be a cruelty to wake him, especially as you've got no news. Now off to bed with you too. You've barely a couple of hours before you're up for Mass, and I suppose you'll be wanting to help with the search again in the morning. That poor wee boy, wherever he is. God grant he's safe.'

'Yes indeed Sadie. I could sleep on my feet. And you must be jaded too. I'll just let Jasper in and let's all go to bed.'

I opened the door expecting to see Jasper snuffling there to be let in. He wasn't much of a one for cold night hikes, liked the comfort of his warm house. But no sign of Jasper. I moved out and called quietly, and whistled for him. No point in waking the neighbourhood. Then I heard a plaintive whining, interspersed with short little yaps. As I moved round the corner of the house towards the sound, I saw Jasper obviously puzzled, sniffing around the garage. The garage of course was empty since neither of us had a car. It contained only the usual debris of a household, bits and pieces that someone sometime had hoped might come in useful again.

A shock of alarm ran through me. Daniel. What if Daniel were in there? I called Jasper to heel and gently opened the garage door. Dark blackness faced me. I lit a match looking for a light switch, and even in its brief flickering glare I could see that our search was at an end. I found the switch and flooded the garage with cold light. Curled up in an old armchair, bits of old curtain wrapped around him, was Daniel. He had obviously just woken, either with the squeak of the unoiled hinges or with the light. His face was a mask of fright.

'Hallo Daniel. You must be frozen stiff in here. Come on into the house, there's some lovely hot soup there. Don't worry about Jasper, he'd never harm a soul, however fierce he looks.'

Daniel shrugged himself clear of the curtains, brushed the lank black hair out of his eyes, and stood up shivering. I put a protective arm round him and led him towards the house. Sadie, sensing that all was not well, had come out also. She took Daniel over without a word, brought him into her snug warm room, poked up the remnants of the fire.

'Just sit there a minute Daniel, and I'll get you a cup of soup. You do like soup, do you?' Daniel nodded mutely. He was petrified with cold or fear or both.

'I'll tell you the best thing Daniel. It's nearly five o'clock now, and I've got to say Mass at seven. So why don't you have your soup and then go and have a good sleep in my bed? Sadie, Miss Nails, will have it lovely and warm. And your parents can come and get you much later on when you've had a good rest.'

His eyes filled with tears and he said nothing. Sadie came in with the steaming cup of soup. 'There now poor lamb. You must be nearly dead, lying out in that freezing garage on a night like this. Drink this slowly now.'

'Daniel's going to sleep in my bed Sadie. I'll ring everybody and put their minds at rest. And when you wake up in the morning we can have a good old chat before you go home. Drink your soup now and I'll get the 'phoning over.' I should have rung Mr and Mrs Lercaro first but for some reason I didn't. Tom agreed to come straight down even though it was fairly certain that the worst that would afflict Daniel would be a chill. The police were happy that the boy had been found. I didn't think there would be any further enquiries that they need make, but I would let them know later.

'Lercaro,' barked the anxious voice of Daniel's father.

'Father Kennedy. We've found Daniel, Mr Lercaro.'

'Thank God. Where was he? Is he alright? Has he been hurt?'

'Calm down Mr Lercaro. There's nothing wrong with him except perhaps a chill. He was lying in a chair in our garage. He's too cold, tired, and frightened to answer any questions just now. As a matter of fact, I took the liberty of putting him to bed here in the presbytery. We'll find out what, if anything, is wrong with him in the morning. The doctor's here now, just checking him over. So yourself and your wife can ease your worries now and go to bed. It's very very good that we found him. I'm so very glad for you.' I could hear Mr Lercaro relaying this information to his wife. Then her soft authoritative voice took over the phone.

'You're quite sure he's alright Father?' I assured her that to every appearance he most certainly was. 'You are so very kind Father. Thank you for everything. I told you he thought the world of you, so I'm perfectly sure he'll be safe and sound in the presbytery. Tomorrow will be time enough to talk about it.'

'Perhaps if you could come down some time in the afternoon Mrs Lercaro? He'll be fully himself again by then.'

'I will, I will Father. Goodnight and thank you again.' She rang off. I was very relieved, as I was sure that Mr Lercaro was about to insist that Daniel came back there and then to the family home. Mrs Lercaro had firmly taken the decision into her own hands, and whatever the truth of their relationship and its effect on Daniel, I was grateful to her for that. I was suddenly immensely tired, as I knew was everyone else who had taken part in this harrowing night. Jennifer with her bright happy humour and willing helpfulness sprang to my mind. I shrugged and went into Daniel.

Tom had just arrived, and after a cursory examination pronounced the boy free from any major ailment. A quick pill and we hastened him off to bed. Sadie reassured Father Morrison who had woken with the bustle, and then helped me to get Daniel into my warm welcoming bed. His eyes closed before she left the room, and though I sat for half an hour or so to make sure he didn't waken in alarm in a strange bed, there was not a flicker or a movement from him. Poor Daniel, I sighed, as I went down the stairs.

After Mass, at which I passed the word that Daniel was found, and that therefore we would need no more searchers, I stretched out for a few hours in a spare room. When I awoke, I went in to Father Morrison, and asked him if he would deal with the Lercaros. Whatever could be, or needed to be, said would come much better from a mature priest rather than from my naïve and inexperienced lips. I apologized for adding to his burdens.

'Don't be even more silly than you have to be, boy,' he said with an undertone of real anger. 'Sometimes you addle me. It's no burden at all, not in your sense anyway. The only burden, I'm afraid, is that I'm likely to get absolutely nowhere. One idea has occurred to me, if you'd be prepared to consider it. The boy apparently likes you. Now if it would work, or even be possible, I wonder if somehow you could take him under your wing, perhaps train him to be an altar-boy, teach him Latin or chess, or any damn thing that would take him out of that house for as often and as long as possible. I can't *ask* you to do it, but it might just go some way to sorting out the poor little beggar's problems.'

Very hesitantly I agreed at least to try. What little confidence I had gained under Father Morrison's gentle kindness, hardly, I thought, extended to taking on the role of surrogate father. But I would try. 'As a matter of fact I'm just about to try my hand at golf, so if you wouldn't mind my spending a couple of hours a few evenings a week, or even on a Saturday I could take him with me. Perhaps we'll make a Henry Cotton of him.'

'Fine, fine. Well perhaps you'd better wake him up and have a chat before his parents come. Have a bite of lunch with him in Sadie's place. Two of us and our dining room would tongue-tie him altogether, I dare say.'

But although he was more alive and less frightened, he either could not, or would not, offer any explanation of why he had run away. He would not even admit to being unhappy at home. It was just something that he'd done on the spur of the moment. He brightened up when I suggested that he came down in the evenings to practise being an altar boy, and even more when the golf was mentioned. Could he have the occasional wallop? Indeed he could.

Poor Father Morrison could get little further with the Lercaros. Even when he put it straight to them, that something might be seriously wrong with their marriage, and that Daniel's odd behaviour was a direct result, Mrs Lercaro closed completely in on herself, and Mr Lercaro positively exploded. 'How can a priest know anything about what goes on in a marriage? How can anybody else know what goes on between two people? It's our life and Daniel's our responsibility, and we'll do what we think is right.'

Resignedly Father Morrison had to accept his stance. But he did put to them the suggestion, about me, and rather to his surprise, they gladly accepted the idea. So, with Daniel's thanks and assurance to me that he wouldn't do anything foolish again, ringing in my ears, I saw them off in their Daimler. Daniel looked very forlorn but there was some hope in his deep unfathomable eyes. I forced Sadie to go to bed for the afternoon, and collapsed gladly into my own.

## CHAPTER SIXTEEN

JENNIFER waited behind for me after Mass on Sunday. I always went out to the church door after I had taken off my vestments, and passed the odd word with those who lingered. When they were all moving off, she came up to me.

'I have to go back tomorrow Father. My leave's up and Margaret and the children are beginning to pull themselves together. I'll be down regularly anyway, probably at the weekends, as I don't work a shift system yet.'

'Well, it's been very nice of you to come, and I can see what a difference you have already made to the family.' I put out my hand to bid her farewell with a strange sense of loss. I would miss Jennifer even though I had been in her company only briefly and on a few occasions.

'Margaret tells me your father and mother live somewhere near York and I know Monday tends to be the day that priests have as their day off. Would you think it impertinent of me to offer you a lift tomorrow? I'm leaving about nine or half past. If that's any use to you then you are most welcome.' She smiled rather embarrassedly and looked away.

'It's most kind of you Jennifer. I'd be delighted to accept your offer. It can be very awkward and take an awful time to get from here to York. I don't go every week, but I was intending to go tomorrow.' My heart was beating just a little faster. It was relief at being saved the long journey by public transport, that's all it was.

'Good. Then I'll call for you about nine to quarter past. Or would you prefer to come to the house?'

'No,' I replied in some puzzlement. 'I'll wait here for you. It's on the way isn't it. Saves my legs, what? Is that alright?'

'Yes, yes Father. It was just that I . . . oh never mind. See you in the morning.'

It was an odd exchange with undertones which I did not understand. But the prospect of pleasant company and a straightforward journey brought a sense of happy anticipation, which quite overshadowed any nagging worries. I would be home much earlier and thus able to spend much more time than usual with my parents. It would be such a relief to unwind after the tiring strain of Daniel's disappearance. He had been down to me twice since his return, and being the bright lad that he was, had already picked up the essentials of being an altar boy. In fact there were several of them who were similarly apprenticed. Since Willie was among them, with his penchant for doing everything wrong by instinct, the presence of Daniel was a source of great relief. I used to walk him back to his house after the practices, but though he prattled freely and apparently happily, we had still never touched on the dark memories of that long night. Patience I thought. Give it time, and perhaps the full story, if there is one, will come out. Meantime, I had arranged with him to accompany me to a nearby field after school some days, so that I might begin my career as a golfer. I had no great hopes of success.

The Sunday passed as Sundays do. Father Morrison was still not strong enough to do his normal share, and especially with the extra preaching that hence devolved on me, I found Sundays a burden. I looked forward to my Mondays off with extra anticipation. Perhaps I had been wrong about my slighting thoughts on holidays. Perhaps we do need regular and sometimes prolonged breaks from our normal routines. I shrugged philosophy aside and simply basked in my hopes of the morrow.

Promptly at nine fifteen I saw Jennifer's car approaching, and went out to join her. It was a fresh sunny morning and the world, even in Brimley, looked at its best. We chatted happily all the way to York. Her work, her hopes, Daniel, her niece and nephew, all were treated by her with a mixture of shrewd observation and humour. No pomposity. This was not just a feather-brained beauty, but a highly intelligent woman. Rarely in a very long time had I enjoyed a conversation so much.

'Do you realize Father,' she said as we drew near to York, 'that we've not directly said one single thing about you. Oh,

I've learned a lot about you just listening to your thoughts about everything else. But what about you yourself? What are your hopes and ambitions?'

'Well . . . er . . . well . . . I've never really given much thought to that Jennifer. As a priest, one's future is moderately certain. I'll go on being a curate, probably in a few different places, for fifteen to eighteen years, and then I suppose I'll be a parish priest, though God help the parish that gets me. So I presume there aren't any hopes and ambitions, as you put it. We give these up, more or less, when we accept Ordination.' There was a silence in the car. I was sure that if Jennifer had not been keeping her eyes on her driving, those candid deep blue eyes would have been fixed on me quizzically. I began to feel rather uncomfortable. 'You see . . .' I said.

'Now look here . . .' she said at the same time. I yielded.

'Before I offer any comments on that view of life, may I just ask you why it is that you so consistently run yourself down? None of the people who spoke to me in Brimley think of you in anything like the way you think of yourself. They see you as immensely kind, hard working, and with a refreshing innocence, or at least lack of any guile or pretence. No, don't blush and bluster. I rather think their view is much more likely to be right than yours.'

I reached for my handkerchief and blew my nose strongly. Even the new glasses I now had slipped under that kind of pressure. I pushed them back up my nose in some confusion.

'Think about it Father, please do. It's the same with this lack of hope or ambition as you put it. I didn't mean were you expecting to become a Monsignor or a Bishop, or have the biggest parish, or anything stupid like that. Only the small and selfish ones I'm sure think in those terms. I mean . . . oh, what did I mean? You are a man, you know, first and foremost Father, and every man should have some idea of what kind of a person, leading what kind of a life, he would wish to be. I didn't, and don't, expect a pat flippant answer. I don't think you're that kind of a person. But please, at least for me, do sometimes think about life, and not just an endless series of people to be visited, parishes to be served, jobs to be done.' There was a quiet intensity about her which was very disconcerting. She broke the solemn mood with a gay laugh. 'I'm sorry Father. I've quite put you out. I'm a nosey bitch and Monday morning, especially such a lovely Monday morning, is no time for sententious phrase making. Please forget my stupidity.'

I asked her to drop me at the bus station where I could get the local bus to the little village where my mother and father lived.

'I've never had such an exhilarating journey home,' I said. 'Please don't apologize. Apart from being so kind in giving me a lift, you really have opened my eyes. I don't know what to say. But at the very least, thank you very much. I hope you have a good day at work, whatever that means. Lots of arrests or something, I suppose.'

We parted laughingly, but on the short bus journey to Kingsmill, and repeatedly during the gentle relaxing day picking up all the news from my parents, her words went round and round in my head. Was I deficient in some way? Did other priests have hopes and ambitions? And if so, what? I became almost annoyed with myself because I could think of no answers. I wasn't even sure what the questions were. Shruggingly I felt that I had stumbled like Alice into a world that didn't make sense to me. I went down to the village square in the evening to get my bus, feeling edgy after what should have been a day of unwinding.

Waiting near the bus stop was Jennifer's little blue car.

'Get in Father. I've finished for the day, and I've nothing better to do, so I thought I'd round things off, by running you back to Brimley.' She was not in uniform, so I presumed that she'd had time to change.

'You can't do that Jennifer. I'll get out in York and just get my train as usual to Barnsley. It's a long way down there, and then you've got to get all the way back.'

'I'd like to do it Father. I enjoy driving, and if I don't take you to Brimley, I'll just sit in my wee pokey flat and get gloomy. So you're doing me a favour. I enjoy your company, it's a nice night, and what better could I do?'

'Well, if you're quite sure. But I do feel it's an awful

imposition. You really don't have to, Jennifer. I never expected that you would.'

'Oh stop bellyaching Father, if you'll forgive me. Sit back and enjoy it. I'm certainly going to.' She laughed happily and infectiously. Suddenly I felt enormously pleased. What a difference from the normal dreary round of bus, train, bus. I laughed loudly too.

'Well then,' she said, 'what shall we talk about tonight?'

She proved just as entertaining a companion in the darkness of the night as she had in the glory of the morning. The miles slipped by in drowsy content. We were still some miles from Barnsley, and hence even more from Brimley, when Jennifer slowed down, pulled into a long drive, and up to the front of what had obviously been a fine country mansion at one time. It now proclaimed in tasteful lighting that it was the Northbridge Hotel.

'I've called in here a few times on my way down to Margaret's. It's a very nice quiet hotel, and I feel so good that I'd love to have a reflective drink. How about it Father? Will you join me?'

'I've never been in a hotel for a drink. Do you think it will be alright, me a priest and everything? I'm sure everybody will stare at us.'

'Oh, don't let's be bothered what other people think,' she trilled happily. 'Besides, any time I've been in here, there have never been more than four or five others. They do a lot of meals, I believe, but the bar seems deserted. And I think you'll like it. It's quiet, tasteful and cosy. Just like you.' She gave me a playful dig in the ribs. 'Come on, be a devil.' The incongruity of that remark sent her into one of her peals of laughter. Slowly, reluctantly, and then as near full-bloodedly as I could manage I joined in.

'Why not? You really are an astonishing woman, Jennifer. I've never met anyone quite like you. Just as well for my peace of mind I think. Come on then, I'll buy you a drink. It's the very least I can do to express my thanks.'

The large entrance hall fulfilled all Jennifer's predictions. Quietly lit, beautifully carpeted and furnished, it projected a delicate sense of an age gone by, an age of leisure and good living. The bar opened to the left of the lounge. A log fire burnt comfortably in a large ornate fireplace. Low armchairs sat pleasantly and informally around exquisitely carved tables. The lighting was discreet, the décor more like that of an old-world cottage, than a modern hotel. Around the fire sat two middle aged couples who did not even look up from their drink and conversation as we went in. We sat in a corner away from them. The barman came for our orders.

'I'll have a gin and tonic please.'

'Yes, yes I'll have one also please. Two gin and tonics please.'

'Certainly sir. Ice and lemon I presume?'

'Yes, yes please.' He moved quietly back to his bar. 'I've never had a gin and tonic. Seen other priests have them. But I don't really drink. Just a few whiskys.' This reminded me of my disastrous evening at the Broadbents'. I told Jennifer about it, and was absurdly pleased at her gurgling reaction. We had a second drink. The time passed in blissful content.

'Good heavens, it's half past ten. And you've got to get back all the way to York.'

Reluctantly we rose from our table, bade the barman goodnight and went out. We said very little on the last lap to Brimley, but it was a comfortable silence.

'I'll drop you here,' said Jennifer abruptly as we neared the house. 'Thank you very much Father. It's been a lovely day. Goodnight.'

'Goodnight . . . er . . . and thank you Jennifer. That's the best day off I've ever had. Goodnight.'

She gunned the car into a quick circle, gave a last wave and was away into thc night. I went to my bed and slept like a log. Frequently during the week my mind returned to that Monday and to the disconcerting and yet enlivening conversations we had had. On the Sunday, I was surprised and yet not surprised to find her again waiting after Mass.

'Same arrangement as last week Father? I don't start again until Monday afternoon.'

'That will be lovely Jennifer. I look forward to it.'

It was as though the last week's conversation had never been interrupted. We seemed to be exactly on the same wavelength. In the evening Jennifer arranged to meet me at the bus stop rather earlier, so that we could relax more at length in the Northbridge, not drinking any more, but just enjoying each other's company. The same two couples sat around the fire, the same barman served us the same drinks. All that was different was the increased understanding we developed, the awareness of the closeness of our tastes and interests.

'Same time next week Father? I know that I'm free Sunday and Monday morning at least next week.'

'See you then, my dear. Goodnight and thank you again.'

Father Morrison's door was open as I went in. He called me. 'Thought you might like a little night-cap to round off your day. Whisky?'

'Well, I've just had a couple of gins Father. Will whisky mix?'

'It will of course, but if you've been drinking gin, its there too. You know where it is, help yourself.'

We sat sipping our drinks. Father Morrison looked old and very tired. 'Nice girl that Jennifer,' he said. 'I'm sure she's very good company.'

'She's been very kind and a great help to me. And she really is astonishingly interesting. And very good fun.'

'Father, in some ways it's none of my business, but forgive me if I say something. An old man always likes to impress others with his wisdom. It would not surprise me if both you and Jennifer were in the first stages of falling in love. I've seen it happen so many times. Young priest tired and lonely for company. Young attractive girl finding in the young priest someone gentle and intelligent. No badness on either side, and then, wham! They find that they're in love. Then it becomes so sad and painful. Whatever they do. Either to break if off, or break the vows and go away. Only sorrow comes of it. Poor Dermot. I really am pouring on the old man act. But think about it, and if you would take my advice, just ease it off before anyone gets hurt. I'm sure you can do it gently and without offence. And believe me, it will be far more difficult and painful later on.'

I struggled with amazement and then anger. And then

realization. 'I'd never thought about it Father. Or to be more honest, I had deliberately avoided thinking about it. I knew I enjoyed her company, and I knew I was looking forward to Mondays, and I just didn't want to probe below that surface. Looking back I think she must have had the same sort of feeling. Justifying it to ourselves, by saying it was just a convenient arrangement.' A heaviness and gloom settled over me. I supped my gin as Father Morrison sat still and silent in his armchair.

'She really is terribly attractive. And though I know nothing about it, I'm sure you're right Father. I could fall in love with her. And that would be so cruel, for her, for my parents, for you and all the good people here in Brimley. I'm sorry to have been so stupidly blind.'

'Don't Father, don't. It all sounds so easy and straightforward in the books, doesn't it? It's only when it begins to happen, that we begin to realize what celibacy is. Not giving up something bad, or even something that doesn't really matter, but giving up the very centre of life itself. I often wonder if the Church is right about this celibacy business. But . . . but, we're stuck with it, at least for now, and this is the only way to tackle it. At least nobody will ever be able to say, as that silly man Lercaro said, that we don't understand. We do Father. You will even more, from now on. You'll know the joy and the love that could have been for you. You'll appreciate it in others. And there'll always be that sadness at the heart of you. It's from that your strength will come.' A long sigh escaped from him. I wondered what memories of lost almost forgotten happiness lay behind his words.

'I'm so very grateful to you Father. I've arranged to go up again next Monday and on the way I'll make some excuse about the future. Golf or something. And then I won't see her any more.'

'It's a painful business, growing up as a priest Dermot. When you get to my age you almost forget what it was like. But you're a fine brave boy. You'll never regret it. The peace of mind you'll have will outweigh all the sense of loss.' He shook himself slowly, rose from his armchair, put away the whisky and the gin. He rested his arm briefly and with gentle kindness on my shoulder. 'Goodnight Father. I'm very tired. Will you put out the lights for me?'

'Yes, of course Father. Goodnight and thank you again.'

I sat with an almost physical ache through me. It was so easy to say, but never actually to see Jennifer again, or to talk and laugh and think with her? The world seemed very empty as I put out the lights and went to bed.

The heaviness was still with me as Jennifer drew up to the door on the following Monday. Even the weather seemed to reflect my mood. It was grey, misty and drizzly.

'You've been thinking the same thing as I have, haven't you Father. Well, don't worry, I'm going away. I knew what was happening, even though I don't think you did. So rather than hurt us both in a way that we'd never get over, I applied for a transfer to the Metropolitan Police, to London. I was interviewed this week and accepted. I begin next Monday. I don't think even now you'll ever know how much I'll miss you. Even these silly bits of days, which are all we've had. I'll keep them always locked in a little corner of my heart.' There was the hint of a sob in her voice, a blinding mist of tears in my eyes.

'I really didn't know what was happening my dear. I'm so sorry, please forgive me.'

'Forgive you,' she said with vehemence. 'Oh dear Father, can't you understand that I shall be happy through my life if only for this memory. Forgive you.'

We tried to talk non-committally for the rest of the journey but it was a hollow pretence on both our parts.

'I won't come for you tonight Father. I don't think I could bear that. Please get out of the car and walk away. Goodbye.'

As if in a trance I opened the door, got out and walked away. I didn't even look back.

# CHAPTER SEVENTEEN

It was by now too dark to take Daniel into the field any longer to practice my golf. It was time I hit the big-time and actually went on to a golf course. I rang Father Fairey, the only other curate whom I knew in the district and asked him if he played golf, and if he'd mind taking me, a complete novice, out on the course with him some time.

'Sure, Dermot. Only snag is that I can't be too long away from here. Got to keep an eye on Father Clancy. Tell you what. I'll pick you up next Monday afternoon, we can have a quick round at the golf course here, and then you could come in and have your tea with us. How's that?'

'That's very kind of you Jim. I'll be waiting for you.'

In the course of the conversation Jim had informed me that he played off eight. I wasn't quite sure what it meant, but it sounded impressive. I had been more zealous with my practice, this past couple of weeks, as at least a partial distraction from my moonings over the loss of Jennifer. At least now most of the time I actually made contact with the ball, but the results were rarely spectacular.

'Keep your head down Father.'

'Left arm straight Father.'

'Don't swing too fast Father.'

'Shut up Daniel and let me get on with it.'

Daniel knew far more about the game than I did, and even with the clubs unreasonably long for his size, seemed to make effective contact with the ball far more frequently than I did. It was sickening. But with the lunatic optimism without which no golfer would ever progress, I convinced myself that since on some occasions I seemed to hit the ball correctly, it was only a matter of good fortune and I would hit the ball correctly every time.

As I warmed up in the field on the Monday morning, the conviction grew stronger. On the course, with real fairways and real holes, all my expertise would coalesce into a round to be remembered.

It was a blustery, overcast day when Jim Fairey arrived to transport me to doom or glory. As I studied his squat simian form it seemed impossible that such a body could hit a ball further and more accurately than could my long sinewy one. I brushed aside my lack of co-ordination in ordinary life. That would disappear on the course, as I whipped my six foot odd into a lethal attack on the innocent ball.

'Got your shoes?' asked Jim.

'Shoes? What shoes? I've got these shoes that I'm wearing. Won't they do? Do you wear special shoes?'

'Oh my God! You don't even know about golf shoes? I'll see what I can do in the locker room. Maybe there'll be an old pair that will fit you.'

'But why do I need golf shoes?'

'Because your feet will go from under you if you don't. You've got to have spikes or some adhesive substance to keep your feet on the ground. I'm beginning to regret coming with you. You're liable to be a danger to yourself if not to everyone else. Oh never mind, it'll do me good to help you.'

My buoyant hopes had all gone by the time we reached the locker room. It was with distinct apprehension that I faced the prospect of the long eighteen holes.

'There's a pair,' said Jim, poking under the low cubicles. 'They're covered in dust, haven't been used for ages, nobody'll mind. What size do you take?'

'Nine, nine and a half. They look about right. Thanks Jim.'

They just fitted, and as they rang on the concrete, they put a little heart back into me.

'You'll need a trolley. You'll find you're tired enough whacking the ball, without carting the bag of clubs on your shoulder as well.'

So I paid green fees and for a cart, and at least, I thought, *looked* reasonably competent, as we walked to the first tee. Jim's sweater was a brilliant green, while I more prosaically had settled for the only one I had, a black one. The breeze ruffled our hair.

'I'll go off first and perhaps you'll pick up a hint or two watching me. Remember, head down, left arm straight, slow swing.'

Daniel's words came to haunt me as I watched Jim tee up his ball, limber up with a few practice swings, and then crack the ball with a blurred swing from which I picked up nothing. Obviously his odd physique was no barrier to good golf. My more regulation body was, I feared, very much less geared to success. Tentatively I placed my ball, fixed my eye unswervingly on it, slowly swung back my club, left arm excruciatingly straight and in a full-blooded swing crashed the club into the ground a foot behind the ball. My wrists felt as if they were broken, waves of pain ran up to my shoulders, tears came to my eyes.

'Very good swing,' said Jim. 'Just bent your arm a bit. Stand up a bit straighter, you'll be fine.'

I repeated the hypnotic movements. This time I would hit the ball. I very nearly did too, except that at the last minute, my hands slipped from the club, which went cartwheeling twenty yards down the course. The ball looked up at me mockingly.

'Perfectly straight. See where the club went. Just get your grip a little firmer. See, I'll show you.' And he did. After I had collected my club from where it lay ignominiously on the fairway, he interlaced my left first finger, with my right little finger.

'Agony,' I wailed. 'I can't possibly swing a club with my hands like that.'

'Yes you can. It'll hold your hands firm, your club straight. Try the swing again now.'

To my surprise, this time the club head made contact, and the ball sailed respectably down the fairway. Nowhere near as far as Jim's, but at least on the way. By the time I reached Jim's ball I had taken another six shots, nearly dislocated my fingers, hacked several great lumps out of the ground, and uttered more oaths than I thought I knew. All of which was made more galling by Jim's easy wallop which landed his ball comfortably on the green. I picked my ball up in disgust.

'That's no way to learn. You've just got to keep at it.'

'But it must be terrible for you watching me hacking away like this. Besides it would take us twenty four hours to get round.'

'Look, play out this hole, however long it takes and then play the odd shot or even the odd hole. We'd better do only nine anyway. As I said, I want to get back.'

So down went my ball again. And the thrashing, missing, digging and swearing were repeated. When I finally tapped the wretched ball, now looking like a war victim down the hole, I had swung, if not connected, all of twenty times. It was an easy par four hole. For the rest I played just the odd shot to keep my eye in, missing the ball as often as hitting it.

The ninth hole led back to the club house. Here, Jim persuaded me to have another go at a hole. To both his and my surprise it took me no more than three shots to be just short of the green. With some honour restored, I took my number eight iron out to chip onto the green. What happened next is still a mystery to me. I swung, connected, and was about to look for the ball on the green, when away to my right there was a shattering of glass.

'You've done it now Dermot. That's a hole in one straight into the members' bar.'

With some trepidation I approached the broken window, the sash of which was firmly raised as I reached it. The man who poked his head through was slim, greying, military looking. I recoiled.

'I say, are you the chappie who put that ball through the window?'

His tone was mild. I nodded silently.

'Well just look what you've done. The ball bounced once and then landed straight in my whisky. Didn't even break the glass, hardly spilt any of the whisky. Bet you couldn't do that again what! When you've finished your round, come in and I'll buy you a drink. Bloody astonishing shot.' He closed the sash down again, and with relief I turned to join Jim who had been observing at a distance.

'Bloody fellow never even gave you your ball back,' he said with a grin.

'What about the window. Hadn't I better pay for that?'

'They didn't seem to be worried, why should you be? We paid for a full round and only played half, so I reckon they got a bargain, window and all. Come on, let's get changed and away before they change their minds.'

'I'm sorry you had such a poor day,' I said as we drove away from the course. 'It wasn't much fun for you.'

'Nonsense. It was a good breath of air and just enough. It's very difficult you know, I dare only stay away a few hours at any time. Paddy Clancy is quite a handful. It's all well and good for that lot at the conference to be very tolerant, lift him up to bed when he passes out, sympathize with him. But day in day out it's very hard work. I have to watch him like a hawk. Like all drunks or alcoholics, he's very sly, and I never know when he's going to get some booze from somewhere, stash it until I'm out, and then get plastered. The worst is when he doesn't pass out, because then he's capable of anything. Great pity. It's hard to know what to do with him.'

As with so many other things, it had never struck me how difficult it must be to cope with a person who is determined, in a kind of childishness, to get drunk whenever he can. Like my golf, I thought ruefully, I go on doing it even though every stroke is a disaster. Did Paddy Clancy I wondered, ever hope to get better? Or did he just go on, as I probably would at golf, accepting inferiority? My respect for Jim Fairey increased.

'I was just thinking, for instance,' he said. 'Suppose we'd had that pit disaster that you had. We could you know quite easily. Same sort of mine, same dangers. I'd be really stuck what to do. If I had to spend the whole night at the pit as you did, Paddy would somehow get hold of some booze and stupefy himself. And if he didn't have enough, he'd be just as likely to roll down to the pit, and make an exhibition of himself. Can you imagine what that would do to the grieving relatives? And yet if I didn't stay there, it would cause, and rightly cause, just as much anger and misunderstanding. It's the devil and the deep blue sea, all the time.'

'You can't go on forever like this Jim. How long have you been here now? Two years?'

'Well, between you and me, I've asked the Bishop for a

move. He's coming down to us for Visitation and Confirmation of the children, the week before he comes to you, and he said he'd talk to me then. I honestly don't think he'll get anybody else to do what I've done. And that will mean that Paddy will have to be put away in some form of institution. It's awful you know, the poor little man. Not his fault I suppose, but we can't just go on propping him up. He's doing little good here, and he's stopping me doing anything much, most of the time. So what do you do?'

I pondered this impossible question as we drove into his drive. 'Are you sure it will be alright in the circumstances for me to bother you for tea? I mean you, and I'm sure the housekeeper, have enough on your hands without the burden of an extra one.'

'Don't be daft. When he's not on the booze, Paddy's excellent company and he'll be delighted to have you. I'm sure he's fed up with my ugly mug, particularly remembering all the times that he knows I've picked him up and put him to bed. He was very pleased when I told him you were coming. Don't worry at all. We'll talk about your appalling golf. Give him a laugh eh?'

Despite these assurances, it was with some trepidation that I went into the presbytery. Similar in construction to ours, it was very much more functional in furnishing. It was impersonal, and had none of the warm welcome that St Aloysius' had.

'Come in, come in Father,' said little Father Clancy. 'You're most welcome. It's not much of a day, so I got a drop of whisky in for the pair of you, to warm you up before your tea.'

Jim and I exchanged wary glances. As if he'd seen them, even though his back was to us, he continued rapidly. 'Don't worry Jim, I haven't taken a drop, nor am I going to. I suppose you know something of me Father, and what a burden I am to everybody, especially to Jim. Well, believe it or not, I'm going to do something about it. Come and sit yourselves down and get warm. Jim you pour the drinks. I don't think I'm strong enough to do that yet.'

He sat down himself, a tiny figure in a huge old armchair.

His feet, as I remembered from the conference, still dangled a couple of feet from the ground. A gentle, sad smile spread over the thin refined features. I felt a catch in my throat.

'I hope you don't mind Father, if I burden you with all this. You're a young man with all your life before you, and you shouldn't have to face up to silly old men like me. But since you gave me the opportunity to do what I've done, maybe it'll do you some good to hear it. I don't know, but bear with me.'

As if he sensed what was going to be said, Jim turned to Paddy and in a voice subdued beyond his normal abrupt roughness said, 'Are you sure you wouldn't just take one? Be no harm at all. Would you?'

'Thanks Jim, but no all the same. It's a silly thing, but perhaps this is the turning point. You see Father, when I knew Jim was going out golfing with you, I got a taxi up to the Bishop. I'd made an appointment of course. And I told him that it was no use going on as I was, with Jim tied hand and foot to me like a nursemaid. I know what you've been through, Jim. I've been so ashamed, so frightened, that I've never been able to express my gratitude to you. Anyway I told His Nibs that I wanted to sign myself into St Hilda's, near York. It's a cross between a mental home, an alcoholics' retreat and a geriatrics' graveyard, you know Father. It's that last bit that will help me if anything does. The thought of sitting round watching those doddery old priests drifting towards the tomb, is enough to stop me drinking forever.'

You'll make it, God bless you, I thought. Anybody who could laugh in that situation had to have guts and enough.

'So, as soon as the Bishop has been here in a fortnight, I'm away. I'm giving myself this fortnight as a real test. If I can pass that, then maybe somehow, sometime I can make it altogether. I've just been terribly selfish for this long time. And I had him so taken aback, that I slipped in the demand that you be left here as parish priest, Jim. If any man ever deserved it, you do. He agreed, to my great surprise. So there it is. I'll never be back here anyway, even if I do get over this. I wouldn't want to. It has too many sad and shaming memories for me. So don't imagine there's anything temporary about it Jim. St Clare's is all yours, you're not just holding the fort.'

There was total silence. There was nothing I could say, and Jim seemed too overcome to make any comment. His comments of the afternoon, his own request to the Bishop, must have come back at him as though they were a betrayal.

'Come on then, the pair of you. Sup up and have another. It's a celebration not a wake. Eileen's getting us a special tea and for God's sake, cheer up.'

Poor Paddy. He worked like a dog through the meal to keep our spirits up, but neither Jim nor I could rise to the occasion. Afterwards, and very humbly, Jim asked Paddy if he'd mind if he drove me back to Brimley.

'Not at all Jim. And it's been very good to have had you Father. You live somewhere near York don't you? Perhaps you might take it into your heart to drop in and give a poor old drunk a touch of the outside world sometimes. I'd be very happy to see you.'

I shook his hand. I could not for the life of me say a word. As we drove through the night to Brimley my conclusion to Jim came out.

'That's it Jim. If poor Paddy in his state can resolve to stick at it like that, then I'm damned if I'm going to give up in the golf. Not until I can get a ball straight into a whisky glass without bouncing it!'

'Good on you Dermot,' said Jim.

## CHAPTER EIGHTEEN

THE Visitation and Confirmation by the Bishop, which Jim had mentioned to me during our odd golf date, had been very much on our minds. Since it happened only every two years or so, the whole parish was spurred to extra effort to show the Bishop how devoted they were.

'Lot of baloney,' grumbled Father Morrison who had been through it all many times before. 'He knows from the regular returns we make all about the parish, so what's all the fuss about. It's just a Public Relations job with Confirmation thrown in.'

But to me, who had never experienced a Bishop's visitation before, it all seemed very important. The children must all be perfect for their Confirmation, the choir must practise their hymns and anthems until they were of suitably heavenly excellence, the altar boys must know their moves and countermoves until they could do them in their sleep. I drove myself nearly to a breakdown with the impossible task of tying up all these loose ends.

I went round all my sick and housebound preparing them for the Bishop's visit. He liked to see the old people. But they, in the main, were totally unimpressed.

'He's been here before,' said old Winnie of the under-the-bed Guinness. 'What's he want to come again for? I offered him a drink last time, but he wouldn't have it. Too snooty, dressed up in all them robes and all. And there'll be all them women of yours in again, tidying me up and making me miserable. Couldn't you tell him I'd died or something? He'd never know. Never care either, I'll bet.'

Joanie Telfer cackled wildly when I told her with due reverence, that she was to be honoured by a visit from the Bishop.

'He won't even know what I mean when I tell him I've had it all out, will he? Them Bishops don't know anything do they? I think I'll tell him what it means and watch him go white.'

I groaned and tried to woo Joanie into a more respectful frame of mind. But however daft she was, she was not daft enough to place any importance on such a visit. So she told me.

'And if you send any of them women in to clean me up, like they did last time, I'll hit 'em with a shovel. I couldn't find anything for weeks after they'd been. Just leave me be, eh?'

What a thankless task. If only the Right Reverend Monsignor Charles Augustus Green knew what he was doing when he made his Lordly wishes clear. What difference could one visit every two years or so, from however elevated a Prelate, do for the likes of Winnie and Joanie? I pulled myself up. I was beginning to share the world-weary cynicism of Father Morrison. What if he was right? I pushed the unworthy thought from my mind, and continued with my preparations.

The choir I was leaving to the excellent guidance of our organist and musician Miss Grimswood. Neither she nor I were under my illusions about their quality.

'I'll just prepare two simple anthems which even they can't ruin, Father. And in the hymns they'll be drowned by the congregation so they won't be noticed there either. Now stop worrying Father, just leave it to me. I rather think the Bishop is tone-deaf anyway, judging by the way he sang last time he was here. And in any case, he's got to listen to them only once every two years. We have that punishment every Sunday. So spare your sympathy for me and the rest of us. Be like Father Morrison, and don't take it all too seriously.'

Nobody was taking it seriously, except me, it seemed. Except me and the altar boys. They were taking it very seriously. Since among others, Willie was numbered in their ranks, that boded good for nobody. When Willie got serious about anything, then disaster could not be far away. Night after night, I drilled them. Where to move, what to do. Night after night Willie was in the wrong place, doing the wrong thing.

'Miss,' he would say to me plaintively, 'why are all them over there, and I'm 'ere?'

'That's alright Willie. You just turned the wrong way. Now come on let's do it again. Willie,' I roared, 'You've done it again. This way.'

'It's that Gregory, Miss. He kicked me as I were turning and made me go t'wrong way.'

'Gregory's nowhere near you Willie. Come on try again. Turn left Willie. Left, not right. Alright, alright, let's leave it for tonight. Back again tomorrow night boys. We've only got a week left, and the Bishop will be very annoyed if we don't do it properly.'

'It's that Willie,' said one of the more angelic and efficient altar boys. 'He never does anything right.'

'I'll smash your bloody face in,' said Willie with very unchristian fervour.

'Now, now boys. No fighting. We're here to serve God and the Bishop, not to squabble. We'll all be fine on the day.'

'Just you keep him quiet, Miss,' threatened Willie, a ferocious scowl on his unprepossessing features. 'Or I'll kill 'im. In front of t'Bishop too,' he added as an even direr warning.

Apart from Willie's ferocity and incompetence, apart from the sheer inability of the rest of them to look reverent and attentive, my main problem was their clothing. In normal parochial functions we never had more than four altar boys performing at any one time. There was a distinct shortage therefore of cassocks, the long black garment, and surplices, the shorter white one, normally trimmed with some form of lace. I approached Father Morrison.

'This,' said Father Morrison grimly, 'is getting out of hand. Do you seriously expect me to spend pounds and pounds on cassocks and surplices which will be worn just the once and then will rot until the Bishop comes again? Sheer waste of money, extravagance, pomp, all those things that the Scripture warns us against.'

Encouraged by the sarcastic glimmer in his eyes, I pressed on. 'Well Father, the ones we have are pretty tatty anyway. It's about time they were renewed. And with altar boys like Willie and the rest, they don't last very long. It's an investment for the future, I suppose you could call it.'

'You're rapidly developing into a very bland hypocrite, young man. Go on, order what you need. You'd better tell 'em to be quick. The wretched Bishop will be here in just over a week. All this ridiculous ceremonial makes me sick. Jesus never wore all these silly robes.'

He was only half joking. This Visitation was doing him no good, and not adding much to my posy of happiness either. At the end of the day, seventy or so children would have been confirmed, and beyond that, all the fuss and palaver would have produced absolutely nothing. I sighed heavily to myself.

The new cassocks and surplices arrived only on the Friday before the Bishop was due on the Sunday. After the frustrating repetition of the altar boys' practice, I summoned them all together.

'Never mind about anything now boys. Even if you forget what to do on Sunday, I'll be there to show you. So just do your best and go where you're told. And now I've got a special treat for you. Since it's such an important occasion,' I winced at my hypocrisy, 'Father Morrison has let me get a whole new set of cassocks and surplices for you to wear on Sunday. So let's go through into the sacristy and try them on. They're of different sizes, so there's sure to be one to fit each of you.'

They were laid out neatly on chairs. The boys rushed past me in a cavalry charge, grabbed the first set they could lay their hands on, and frantically began to fit the robes on their small bodies. Willie, of course, led the attack. Gradually as I calmed them down, and as they buttoned and pulled, the untidy set of ragamuffins was replaced by a sedate almost angelic host. Some had outfits a little too big, some a little too small, and I arranged for them to swop into ones more suitable for their size and shape. Willie, despite being first in the dash, was, as always, the last to complete his robing. His shining face and tousled hair poked out of the smallest cassock of them all. Buttoned at the neck, it was very obviously close to strangling him, and the rest of the buttons were fastened so eccentrically, that the cassock pouched in a series f lumps around his body. The arms stretched to just below his elbows, his rolled-down socks and dirty pumps were at the end of nearly two feet of visible, and very dirty leg. The white surplice was like a scarf around his neck. He had been quite unable to get his arms through the appropriate holes.

'Miss, Miss, is this alright?' he squeaked, his face rapidly reddening.

'No, it most certainly is not Willie. Come here for God's sake before you choke yourself.'

I loosened the top button and the whoosh of air into Willie's lungs could have been heard, I'm sure, in Barnsley.

'Stand still and let me get you out of it before you destroy it.' My patience with Willie was running very thin. I looked round my team. Little Fred Smollett was standing virtuously still in a rather trailing set of robes. He looked for all the world like a cross between Pinocchio and Dopey of the Seven Dwarfs.

'Take yours off Fred. I think this one will fit you better, and perhaps we can stuff Willie more easily into yours.'

The exchange was duly made, not without struggles and sibilantly whispered oaths from Willie. But at least then, he looked more like an altar boy. A very odd servant of the Lord was Willie.

'On Sunday, boys, I want you to be sure to be here in the sacristy at half past two. The Bishop starts the Confirmation service at three o'clock, and we've got to be ready well before he comes. Wash your faces and hands, comb your hair, polish your shoes. We've got to be neat and tidy. And don't worry, you'll all be fine. Goodnight now and God bless you.'

As they trooped into the night Willie hung back.

'What is it Willie? I'm very busy. I've a lot to do.'

'Please Miss,' said Willie in a hoarse whisper. He looked around to make sure we were alone. 'Miss, I haven't got any shoes.' Tears were in his eyes, and bitter remorse in my heart. Here was poor Willie, all on his own, without any help or encouragement from his family, and I was using him as a butt for my own shortcomings.

'I'm sorry Willie. Look, come up to the house after Mass in the morning, and I'll take you down and get you a pair of shoes. It'll be our secret, so don't tell anyone. There's a good lad, off you go.'

I patted his wee tousled head. He gulped. 'I've never had a pair of new shoes, Miss.'

At the shoe shop the next day, the usual chaos followed Willie. He missed the stool in attempting to sit down, and crashed in a swearing heap to the floor. When he removed his battered tennis pumps, his socks were revealed as a series of holes surrounded by a few stray threads. I nodded to the kindly lady that she should sock his dirty little feet, before trying any shoes. Finally having chosen a pair which fitted him, to Willie's unrestrained glee, we left the shop. His eyes were mesmerized so much by the shoes that he walked straight into the nearest lamppost. Not even the painful lump on his head could restrain his ebullient awe.

'Oh Miss, thanks. I've never had a pair of new shoes,' he repeated, and to my intense embarrassment, threw his arms around my legs and kissed the middle button of my jacket.

'You watch me tomorrow Miss,' he said with great pride. 'I'll be the best of the lot.'

I went home glowing with virtue, though the glow diminished rapidly as I paid my last calls to various of my sick. All were still recalcitrant. None of them wanted the Bishop and they'd be damned rather than make any special preparations. If only you knew, Right Reverend Bishop, what a whole lot of disturbance you cause. The only good thing to come out of your visit is Willie's shoes.

Father Morrison too was in very bad humour. 'I'm not going round the parish with him tomorrow. You'll have to do that. Driving up to these poor people's homes in a chauffeur-driven Daimler. Lot of pompous rot. Can't stand it. Can't stand him.'

I was astounded at the effect that the Bishop's visit was having on his normal mild-mannered nature. It became ever clearer that he and his parishioners saw very much more eye to eye about the essentials, than I had ever realized. A true pastor, or shepherd, does feel for his flock and they in turn share his feelings. I seemed a lonely outsider, dashing round making insane preparations for ceremonial that nobody wanted, nobody appreciated. The ways of the Lord, and the Lord Bishop, were distinctly odd. What was annoying, was that despite the additional burden of the Bishop, all the normal routine of the parish Sunday had to be gone through anyway. It was all very well for him, swanning down for his big appearance, but the rest of us had to sweat away as normal. He arrived in time for lunch, which Sadie had prepared with her usual efficiency and skill. Father Morrison grunted his way through the meal, and I sweated in my usual tongue-tied way. The Bishop – I supposed that was part of his training – blandly ignored both our moods, and sailed through, giving us little snippets about Diocesan affairs, which meant, to me at least, absolutely nothing. It was a relief when he rose, appeared to flex himself mentally or spiritually, and spoke with pontifical pomposity.

'Well Fathers, this is all very nice. But it isn't getting the work done. We've got over an hour before the Confirmation, so perhaps I could visit the sick first. It will be better that way, as I'm rather tired after the Confirmation.' *You're* tired, I thought. What about us?

'Father Kennedy will go with you. I'm not very well, you know My Lord. And he knows the parish very well.'

'Fine, fine. Let's go then, Father.'

I have never been sure since whether the Bishop noticed the welcome he received in many of the houses. Either he did and ignored it, or he was so sure of his own value, that he didn't even advert to the situation. Joanie Telfer was positively obscene.

'Father Kennedy knows all about me Your Worship,' she said, with a leer that would have been embarrassing in a strip club. 'I've had it all out you know,' she went on, with a knowing wink. 'Would you like to see for yourself, Your Holiness?' She began to lift her ancient stained black skirt.

'That's perfectly alright, my dear lady,' said the Bishop unctuously. 'If you would just care to kneel down, I'll give you my blessing.'

'Oh good,' said Joanie, lifting her skirt anyway as she shuffled to her knees, revealing a grimy pair of yellow drawers. 'Are you going to put your 'ands on me 'ead like you did last time? I liked that. Gave me a thrill that did.'

When the chauffeur finally delivered us back to the presbytery, it was already after half past two.

'If you'll excuse my, my Lord, I'll just get into the sacristy, and see to the altar boys. I hope you'll forgive any mistakes. They're all very excited and likely to forget what comes next.'

'Don't worry at all Father. We're used to it. My Secretary will take care of everything. I'll just go in and have a word with Father Morrison until three o'clock.'

He beamed paternally at me. I rushed into my cassock, smoothed down my dishevelled hair, and moved into the sacristy.

'Miss, Miss,' I was greeted by Willie. 'Am I alright Miss?'

Willie was standing proudly. His face was shining with virtue and cleanliness, but a very visible tide-mark round his neck revealed where he had begun and ended. His cassock and surplice were at least on in the right order, but already looked as though Willie had slept in them. I straightened them to whatever degree was possible. My eyes strayed to the new shoes. The toes already had been scuffed as though they were three years old.

'You're fine Willie, just fine.' I patted him gently. 'Don't worry about a thing. Just stand over there with the rest of them.'

I lined up my troops. No general had ever faced a battle with an army in whom he had less confidence. I smiled bravely at them. We'd go down fighting whatever else. The Bishop came through and gave them an all-embracing welcome. Their own smiles became a little less confident faced with the vision that was the Bishop. He was a word to them before, now the gloriously garbed reality was upon them. Their feet began to shuffle, their hands to grasp their surplices convulsively. I moved over to them to calm their pre-battle tensions.

'Good boys,' I said quietly. 'You look splendid. And all your families will be proud of you.' Except Willie's, I thought. They won't even be there to see him. 'Now line up in twos. Remember? And just keep your eyes on me. I'll tell you what to do all the time.'

Willie I had carefully placed in the middle, so that he would merely have to follow the rest. That was no guarantee that he would, but it was the best that I could do. The Secretary clicked his official fingers and we moved out into the arena.

In fact, the ceremony was not very complicated, and the boys, though they hardly looked polished performers, made no great mistakes. Even Willie had marched, genuflected, and bowed, like a rather untidy guardsman. I beamed delightedly at them all. The children to be confirmed in their white dresses or neat suits looked suitably pious, the choir sang their simple anthems straightforwardly. We lined up for the final procession.

At this stage, two of my altar boys had to perform their one solo of the afternoon. I had chosen Gregory O'Keefe to take the Bishop's mitre to him which he did splendidly. And simply to make him feel important, I had chosen Willie to present the long crozier or shepherd's crook. Whether it was the new shoes, or sheer nervousness, I never knew. Willie reached the Bishop, tripped spectacularly, but somehow managed to transfer the crozier to the Bishop's hand and to grasp the other hand. He was supposed to kiss the Bishop's ring. But he was in such a state of unequal equilibrium, that all he could do was sink his teeth firmly into the Bishop. A yelp of anguish was torn from the Bishop's sculptured lips, the crozier was jerked spasmodically upwards, neatly dislodging the mitre from his head. He was lucky he didn't lose an eye. Willie worried the finger for a few seconds and finally fell to the floor. I hastened to pick him up and put him in line, before the Bishop kicked him.

The procession moved down the aisle and the parishioners unashamedly grinned. For them at least, if not for the Bishop, the afternoon had been worthwhile.

'Didn't know you bred cannibals in Brimley. Haw, haw,' ventured the Bishop sucking his maimed finger and trying to put a good face on it.

'Miss, I slipped,' said Willie rather unnecessarily. 'Did I do alright?'

'You did very well Willie. You were the star of the afternoon.' He grinned in delight and took his happy little person away. It was all over, and the one disaster had at least come at the very end, and had not disrupted the ceremony itself. I sighed contentedly as I went back into the presbytery for tea. It was to be only a snack and was served in Father Morrison's room. It passed pleasantly enough, and after it, Father Morrison and the Bishop's secretary stood up.

'You'll be wanting to talk to Father Kennedy, my Lord. You may as well stay in here, and Father Jackson and I will find ourselves somewhere else. Would you care for a drink or anything, my Lord?'

'No thanks Father. Good of you to offer. We won't be long, because I have to get back. Thank you for the room.' They left and I sat fidgeting uneasily. I had never had a conversation with a Bishop.

'Well Father, how do you like Brimley then? Mining towns are all the same, very warmhearted, I've found.'

'Yes, yes my Lord. It's fine. I'm fine. I like it very much. Great people.'

'Good, good. You seem to have settled in very well. And how do you get on with Father Morrison? Bit of a difficult man.'

'Far from it my Lord. I've always found Father Morrison wonderfully kind and helpful.'

'Don't interrupt Father. I was about to say that Father Morrison has a history of being awkward. I wanted to move him to another parish. He'd been far too long here. And he just refused to go! Well, short of taking the whole case to Rome, there was nothing I could do. So I left him. Very awkward man. But you get on fine with him eh? Hope that doesn't mean you're going to be awkward too. Haw, haw! Just a joke Father. I'm quite sure you'll be perfectly amenable and obedient. Good then, Father. Any problems at all? Anything I can help in? No? Good. Well God bless you Father. Keep up the good work.'

I bent to kiss his ring and had an insane urge to sink my teeth as well into his well manicured fingers. I choked down my feelings and went to summon Father Morrison. An even greater sigh of relief passed my lips as I watched the Daimler drive away. It was finally over.

'Come into my room and let's have a drink, Dermot. You were marvellous and I'm so glad you trained that little lad to bite him. I've never been happier in my life. I could have rolled on the carpet when I saw him jump. A pretty, pretty sight.'

We scarcely had the drink in our hands when the front door bell began to ring, and carried on ringing. Insanely. And with repeated thumps on the door as well.

'God Almighty, go and see who that is Dermot. It has to be a crisis. Nobody could ring like that for anything ordinary.'

I almost ran to the door, beating Sadie by a short head. There, jumping up and down in excitement, was Frank O'Malley, Kathleen's husband.

'She's had it. It's a boy. And the doctors say it's fine as far as they can see. It *is* a miracle. It *is*.'

'Come in Frank before you burst a blood vessel. We're just having a drink after the Bishop and I'm sure you could do with one yourself.'

'No, I won't Father. Thanks. I'm just rushing back to the hospital. It's a boy did I tell you? Kathleen wants to call it after you. She made me come and tell you.'

'Oh God, not another, tell her not to. I can't go on, if half the children of the parish are called after me.'

'It's amazing Father. She wasn't due until next weekend. We came to the Confirmation and when that little lad bit the Bishop, Kathleen went into such convulsions of laughter that she began to go into labour. We just had time to whip home, get her things and rush her to the hospital. She had it within the hour. Easiest birth they've ever had. Oh Father, even I could kiss you.'

'I'll tell you what Frank. Call it William. That's the name of the wee boy. It will be a fitting remembrance of the occasion. That's what you'll do, call it William.'

'I'll tell her Father. Thanks a lot. Have to go.' He was into his car and away like a flash. I went into Father Morrison, acquainted him with the final event of the day, and we sank our faces in relief and laughter into the whisky.

# CHAPTER NINETEEN

FATHER MORRISON retired early to bed. Despite his experience, and his casual attitude to everything to do with the Bishop's visit, the occasion had obviously been a strain. He looked drained and white.

'Goodnight Dermot. Thanks for everything, especially today. I'm very tired.' Those were the last words he ever spoke to me. I said the early Mass in the morning and was having my breakfast, when Sadie came back into the dining room. A worried frown lay on her face.

'I think Father must have slept in,' she said to me. 'I don't hear any sounds of his getting up, as I normally do.'

'Well, don't worry about it Sadie. I'll give Communion to anybody who comes, and Father can say Mass when he gets up. He needs a rest, and if he's sleeping, well and good.' I turned back to my breakfast and newspaper.

'I know it's silly Father, but I really am worried. I've got a funny feeling that he's not well. Would you, just for me, knock on his door and go in to see that he's alright?'

More amused than annoyed at this interruption, I went upstairs to humour Sadie. I knocked firmly on the door. Not a sound. I opened the door, saying 'Father, Father,' as I moved into the room. The bedside light was on, the bed turned back but never slept in. And kneeling by the bed, still in his cassock as he was the night before, was Father Morrison.

'Father,' I said, going over to him, 'it's time for Mass.'

I put my hand on his shoulder and his body slid slowly to the floor. His flesh was cold and clammy, there was no sign of a pulse. A faint bluish tinge coloured his lips. I jumped back as if shot. He was dead. Father Morrison dead? I backed slowly out of the room.

Sadie was waiting on the landing. She saw the pinched look on my face.

'What is it Father? Is he ill? I knew there was something wrong.'

'Sadie, I'm afraid he's dead. He was kneeling by the side of his bed. Must have just died there last night. Come on downstairs love, and I'll get you something. I'd better ring Tom.'

Tom was round in minutes. After a brief examination, he came down to us. 'Must have been a massive coronary. He obviously knew nothing about it. Died in seconds. Poor Father Morrison. I'm very sorry Sadie, but there could have been no suffering at all.'

Sadie was sitting, a cup of tea cooling in her hands, in a numb state of shock. 'I knew there was something wrong Doctor. I knew it. Poor Father Morrison. He was a good man.' She put down the cup, her face crumpled and great racking sobs shook her thin body.

'There there Sadie. Here, take one of these pills. It'll just calm you down and help you carry on. There'll be an awful fuss. There always is when a priest dies.'

As Tom gave her the pill, I took her hard little hand in mine and patted it ineffectually. 'Poor Sadie. Come on now, darling. It's how he would have wanted to go. No long illness, no fuss. Isn't it incredible though, so soon after getting over the cancer which should have killed him?'

'That's what probably did kill him Father,' said Tom. 'The shock of that fierce operation was just too much for his old heart. God rest his good soul. Look Father, I'll get the undertaker and sort out that side, and I'll make out the death certificates and hand them in. You'll have your hands full enough with the Bishop, and sorting out the funeral lunch. They'll all be here, the priests I mean. Nothing they like better than a clerical funeral.'

'You've been very good Tom. Thanks very much for everything. There's nothing more you could have done.'

'It's the least I could do for a great old soul. Look why don't you and Sadie come up to our place to eat tonight? Maeve and I would be very happy.'

'No thanks Doctor,' said Sadie wiping her eyes. 'I think our place is here, at least until after the funeral.' She looked sadly at me. 'You go if you wish, Father, but I'll stay here.'

'It's very good of you Tom, but I think we'd better stay. Thank you very much anyway. As Sadie says there'll be more call for us here. Thanks again Tom.'

I had never experienced death at a directly personal level, nor had I ever had to organize all the details of a funeral. Even before I rang the Bishop, therefore, I contacted Jim Fairey. I was lucky to catch him. He was in his first full week as the parish priest, and with the departure of Paddy Clancy, he was about to have his first full day off in two years. He gave me the benefit of his advice and said he would come over the following day to help me with any further details.

Then I rang the Bishop. As always with authority, it takes time to get through. A receptionist and his secretary both had to vet me before I was allowed to have words with the big chief. I told him what had happened.

'Good heavens, Father. I had no idea he was so ill. I thought he was quite on the mend. Could it have been my visit, haw, haw?'

'Yes, it very well could,' I interrupted sharply. 'My Lord,' I added grudgingly. 'The doctor says that the strain of the Visitation on top of the operation might very well have caused his heart to collapse.'

'Father, I hope I'm not correct in hearing a note of rebuke in your voice? Nor I hope are you even thinking, let alone expressing, that Father Morrison's death is in any way attributable to me?'

'I do apologize, my Lord. I'm just upset at Father Morrison's death. Of course I wasn't blaming you my Lord. I'm just disturbed.'

Mollified, he began to give instructions for the funeral. Thursday he thought would be a good day. He would be present and preach the panegyric, the farewell sermon over the dead. I had better allow for about a hundred and fifty priests, and arrange for the lunch in a suitable hotel. Couldn't be in Brimley of course, there wasn't one large enough. It was all very businesslike, a far cry from the quiet mourning that I would have preferred, and that I'm sure Father Morrison would have preferred.

First I had to get a small card printed, announcing the death and the arrangements for the funeral, checking first with the undertaker, who had arrived. Then when this rush order had been delivered to me, one card had to be sent to every parish in the diocese. For that I drafted the help of several good ladies, who addressed all the envelopes for me. I had rung a large country house-type of hotel between Brimley and Barnsley, well used to conferences. They agreed to provide the meal, asked me merely to be as precise as I could be about the numbers on the morning of the funeral. And that was it. Father's body had been taken away, all provision had been made for his funeral. So little a time since we had risen from our beds that morning, and we were already in a new and empty world. Sadie and I sat wearily drinking tea. A thought struck me.

'Sadie do you know if Father has any relatives, brothers or sisters, who should know and who might want to come to the funeral?'

'No Father. He was all on his own. He was an only child you know and his parents are long dead. There may be odd cousins, but I wouldn't know. Of course there are his friends in Sicily, but I think a letter to them would be enough. They're hardly likely to want to come all that way, just for the funeral. He was always a bit pushed as to where to go, or who to go with on holiday. He was a lonely man, you know Father. That's why you were so good for him this last year. He liked you, you know. Oh he'd laugh about you, and some of the things you did, but it was a kind laugh, and he once said to me that you were the best of all the curates he'd ever had.'

To cover my embarrassment, I voiced another thought that had come to me. 'What about his papers, Sadie? Don't you think we ought to go through his desk and his drawers. I wouldn't want whoever comes in, to disturb his privacy. I'm sure he'd prefer that we did it. And is there a will, or do priests leave wills? And what happens to all his books and things like that?'

'I don't know about the books or anything Father, or the will. I should take anything you want yourself. There's nobody he'd prefer to have them, I know. And we'll go through the papers tomorrow, and get rid of anything that isn't to do with the parish. We don't want strangers nosing through his life.'

Finally we came to a subject that had been nagging at me throughout the sad day, and all the details that had had to be arranged. 'What about you Sadie? What are you going to do? I don't know who will be appointed to take over from Father, but whoever it is will either have a housekeeper already, or will have somebody in mind. They all seem to, from what I've heard. So what's going to happen to you, love?'

'I've thought of that, Father, during the day, and I'm going to do what I did before, all those years ago after Frank was killed. I'm going to go away again. I'll stay for a week or two if the new priest wants me to, until he can get somebody else. But after Father Morrison, there's nobody else I'd want to be housekeeper for, except you, and you won't be needing one for a lot of years yet, Father. So I'm going to go back to Bristol. I'm still not too old to get a job of some kind and I'll be alright. I've been used to loneliness for a lot of years, as I told you. It was different with Father Morrison, but I'll get over that. Don't worry about me Father. I've some very good years, and some very good memories, and thanks to you I can go back to even longer memories now. Oh, I'll be alright.'

There were tears in both our eyes. I put my arms around her and gave her a great hug. At the end of the day, despite all the parading priests and sermonizing bishops, it would be only Sadie and I whose lives would be really disturbed. Even the parishioners would simply get used to the new priest.

'Dear Sadie. Well, you just remember to keep in touch wherever you are and wherever I am. You hear me!'

I thought of Amos. He would have been working all day, or perhaps sleeping, preparing for a late shift. I must go down to his house, and make sure that he, above everybody, had heard of our loss. So it was an eerie coincidence to hear the door bell ring, and be followed by the strangely light footsteps of Amos coming through. He went straight up to Sadie and put his arms gently around her, rocking her against his huge chest. And then, still without a word, he crushed my hands between his.

'I was just this minute setting off to see you Amos. I didn't want you of all people, not to know.'

'I heard when I came out of t'pit. Anything I can do to help? Not that it really counts. When it's all over, all that matters is that we've lost a good man and a fine priest.' There was a huskiness in his voice.

'Sit down Amos. It was good of you to come. I'll go and get a drink for all of us. I'm sure the parish can stand it, and we all certainly need one.' We sat into the night easing each other's sorrow and loneliness.

For Mass in the morning the church was crowded, testimony to the parishioners' wish to mourn their Father. Most of them would not be able to attend the formal funeral Mass. They would be working. But this was their tribute to the priest whom they had known and respected for so long. It was to be the same on the Wednesday and the Thursday. To me those days of parish mourning far outweighed the official ceremonial of the public funeral. They were wordless occasions. Miners rarely descend to speech to express their deepest feelings.

Less comforting exhibitions of the way things had so suddenly changed, were revealed by the visits of various priests. Officially calling to express their condolences, they were, I very soon found, primarily coming as scavengers. A weaselly ginger-haired Father Wright, who had never to the best of my knowledge, been inside the house, or known Father Morrison, was typical. I left him in Father's room to get him a cup of coffee, and to my horror, when I returned, he was piling up mementoes of his visit, books, pictures, statues.

'May as well get in while there's anything left, eh Father,' he said with a toothy grin. 'You'll have salted away whatever you want.'

I carefully put down the coffee and deliberately loomed my six foot odd over his weedy five foot seven. I didn't have to feign any anger. 'Just leave those exactly where they are Father, and get out. Get out before I kill you too.'

'Who the blazes do you think you are?' he spluttered as he retreated rapidly and empty-handedly from the room. 'Snotty little curate. You just watch yourself.'

I followed him to the front door and slammed it after him. Then I carefully returned the articles to their places, locked the door of Father's room and pocketed the key.

'Quite right, Father,' said Sadie when I told her. 'You'd think they'd have more decency and respect for the dead. But you always get the odd greedy ones. Don't let it upset you Father. Father Morrison used to tell me about it in other parishes. It really used to make him mad. So you can be sure he'll be looking down on you with a chuckle. I'll bet Father Wright won't come looking again in a hurry. You quite frightened me, you looked so fierce.'

Somewhat shamefacedly I said, 'Well, he just got on my nerves. Stealing, that's what it was. Sorry, Sadie, I made such a fuss.'

The funeral itself was very impressive. Priests filled half the church, and work or no work, the parishioners turned out in large numbers. The sermon was warm and kindly, a contrast, rather ironic, to the words said to me by the same bishop only the Sunday before. Everybody walked the short distance to the cemetery, and the local police, who had also sent their formal condolences, directed the town's traffic for us. Through it all I could see and hear the ironic smile and deflating comments which Father Morrison himself would have passed on the occasion. I felt lost. I had little part in the ceremonial and nobody seemed to find it necessary to take me into account. They were quite right of course. Finally as we walked away from the grave, the full realization of my own loss hit me. As well as my worry for Sadie, the question of what would happen to me began to nag my mind.

Any doubts were soon put at rest. Back in the presbytery, the Bishop called me into Father Morrison's room as he was disrobing.

'Sit down Father. I won't be going to the lunch. I never do, you know. So I'd better tell you now what's going to happen, as I won't have the chance later. I've appointed Father Kelly as the new parish priest. Do you know him? No. Well it doesn't matter. I think it's always better for a parish priest to start in a new parish with a new team, as it were. Gives them a better chance to do things their own way. All priests are different, you know, Father. So I'm moving you away from Brimley and sending Father Smith to replace you. Do you know him? No. Well it doesn't matter either. I'd like you to go to Senley, that's a country parish near York. You may know it, you come from near York yourself. You do. Good. Father Forrester is the parish priest. It's a big parish in the sense that it's very scattered, so it'll give you experience of a different kind. I'm very grateful for all the good work you've done here, and for all the help you gave Father Morrison. Father Forrester is a very different kind of man. Strong as a bull. So he'll not be dying on you. Haw, haw. Very good Father. Father Kelly will be coming in on Monday or Tuesday next, and perhaps you could move out by the weekend. It's a straight swop for Father Smith. He's with Father Forrester now. God bless you Father.'

I knelt and kissed his ring. Not a single word had I said. My future was now settled. Did it fulfil any hopes or ambitions, as Jennifer would have said? I didn't know. There was a numbness and apprehension. I told Sadie the news and went off with Jim Fairey to the lunch.

When I returned in the evening, Amos joined Sadie and I again. We felt like the Three Musketeers, about to be split up forever. There was an air of quiet gloom about us.

'Well, that's it,' I said. 'One week and I'll be gone from Brimley. And Sadie too. It seems scarcely any time since I arrived. Wet behind the ears I remember you saying, Amos. I still am I think, but perhaps they're drying off a bit.'

'We'll miss you Father,' said Amos. 'Don't go making promises to people that you'll come back, though. They all do. I'm sure they all think they will. But perhaps one visit and then they get tied up wi' their new place, and that's it. You will too Father, you'll see. It's a funny life you lead as priests, Father. You make friends, real friends, good friends, and then you're whipped away. There'll be other Amoses and other Sadies and you'll have to leave them as well. And we're all the poorer for it, especially you poor lads. It's a pity they just couldn't leave you in the one place like everybody else. But of course if you were stuck with a funny priest, or in a parish you didn't like, that'd be bad too. There's no winning is there, Father!'

'Don't you let him depress you Father. You just be happy wherever you are. There are other places than Brimley, and the few people like Amos, that you want to see again, you will, I know. I think real friends last forever. Even when they're dead. We'll all have Father Morrison with us for the rest of our lives.'

And so we chatted with the shadow of departure dark over our heads. During the week I said goodbye to all my old and sick people. They were much more fatalistically used to partings. For most of them life had been a long series of farewells. They could drag no tears up for yet another. And why, anyway, should they weep for me? The schoolchildren were assembled by Sister Clare to sing their good wishes, and to present me with a little scroll expressing their good wishes for the future. I picked out my own Three Musketeers, Gregory, Daniel and Willie. They would face their problems without me now, and I would probably never know what they made of their lives, or their lives made of them. I blessed them all and wished them happiness. Maeve and Tom insisted that I go up for a farewell drink with them. We laughed, but a little sadly, at the memories of my earlier drinking session. Tom said he was going to get drunk anyway. Maeve patted me and stroked me, and said how much they would all miss me.

'Now don't get annoyed Father at what we've done,' said Tom. 'We know you're going to Senley where there'll be a lot of travelling to do. So we took the liberty of having a bit of a whip round for you, mainly among those who've got a bob or two. And we'd like to give you this cheque with our thanks. It'll buy you a little second-hand car for traipsing around in. Now. Sup up and have another drink. I hate speeches.'

'Tom, Maeve. What can I say? It's so very kind of you. But then you are, and always have been, you big drunken Irish bum.' My voice faltered and I hastily gulped down the remains of my whisky. Mindful of my previous experience, I sipped the next one more slowly, and marvelled at the sheer goodness of people.

Sadie left on the Wednesday. Father Kelly had brought his own highly efficient housekeeper, who obviously needed no hints from Sadie. I went to the station with her.

'I'm so glad you came to Brimley, Father. There's nobody I've ever met who I would prefer to have been with, and I know poor Father Morrison, God rest him, felt the same. So goodbye, my stumbling Father. Just be happy.' She kissed me.

'Goodbye Sadie. Thanks for everything. And keep in touch.'

I walked slowly back to the presbytery. That was it. My few poor goods and chattels were packed and ready for the morrow. My room seemed empty and cold. Jasper had already been given to friends on one of the farms. No Sadie, no Father Morrison, no me. I thought over the people, my people. Nellie and big Matt, still coming to church. Joanie, Amy and the other delightful eccentrics. Willie, Daniel and Gregory. The miners, especially those who had died or were injured for life. Kathleen and Mary, the unexpected mothers. Jennifer away now in the lonely throng of London. They were all part of my life forever, as Sadie had said.

Amos took me to the station. Same station, same car, same Amos. Only I was different. I had grown with the life of Brimley. I would never be the same as that wide-eyed boy who so very little time ago had fallen out of the train.

'Goodbye Amos and God bless. And God bless Brimley too.'

The train moved northwards, away from Brimley.